To Julia
Enjoy the Book!

W9-CBI-604

Visit Annie @
www.themadonnaghost.com
-or-
annietillerymystery.wordpress.com

The
MADONNA
GHOST

LINDA MARIA FRANK

iUniverse, Inc.
Bloomington

The Madonna Ghost

This is a work of fiction. All of the characters, names, incidents, organizations, and dialogue in this novel are either the products of the author's imagination or are used fictitiously.

iUniverse books may be ordered through booksellers or by contacting:

iUniverse
1663 Liberty Drive
Bloomington, IN 47403
www.iuniverse.com
1-800-Authors (1-800-288-4677)

ISBN: 978-1-4401-9074-2 (pbk)
ISBN: 978-1-4401-9076-6 (cloth)
ISBN: 978-1-4401-9075-9 (ebk)

Printed in the United States of America

iUniverse rev. date: 10/24/2010

CONTENTS

Chapter 1
ESCAPE

"HERE, HOLD THIS FOR ME, Annie."

I looked at my aunt Jill with utter disbelief as she thrust two ferry tickets at me. I had a large suitcase in each hand, my roller blades slung over my shoulders, Aunt Jill's tennis racket under my arm, and the car keys she had given me to hold a minute ago between my teeth. I muttered my protest, finding it impossible to get my tongue past the car keys. What came out was more drool than intelligible language. Finally, she looked up from the purse she was digging in to see what the trouble was.

"Oh, sorry!"

With that, she stuck the tickets in my T-shirt pocket.

"Thanks!"

Not feeling very grateful, I hurried after her as she headed toward the ferry station. She was pulling ahead of me quickly, even though she had one bag on a shoulder strap, one under each arm, and one in each hand.

I looked ahead to the ferry station across the coarse gravel parking lot. Through the dust clouds raised by the cars pulling into the remaining spaces, I could see a large, weathered, gray, wooden building, shed-like in appearance. Behind the building, the super structures of two white ferries could be seen, bristling with wispy radio antennas and twirling radar ones. Milling all around the building like colorful ants dislodged from their hill was a crowd of waiting ferry passengers. Like Aunt Jill and me, this busy mass of humanity was bound for Fire Island and a summer vacation.

We arrived at the tiny ticket office and gratefully dropped our luggage to the ground.

"Can I get a ten-ticket pass, please?" I heard Aunt Jill inquire of the ticket agent. This might be a vacation for me, but she was going to have to go back to New York City to check in at work a couple of times a week.

"Ask if the ferry's on time. Okay?"

"They're always on time, Annie, unlike most things in our sweet young lives. Let's find a spot over there on those benches."

Gawking in fascination at the people around me, I stumbled after my confident, determined aunt. I felt like one of those little ducklings following the mother duck. Imprinting is what they call it in biology. I guess I have imprinted on Aunt Jill, or J as I like to call her. It was a special name I came up with, and it made me feel more like her friend than her niece. J is my hero. She's a cop, a special-assignment detective with the New York City Police. She treats me as if I have a few working brain cells, and I can talk to her.

"Annie, do me a favor? Go into that little shop over there and buy four batteries for the camera, will you? It will be twice the price on the island."

J thrust a twenty my way, as she stacked the luggage next to one of the wooden benches we had found.

"Yeah, maybe I'll get some gum, too," I called over my shoulder as I collided with a short, stout, sixtyish woman. She was cradling a Lhasa apso puppy in each arm, so she couldn't adjust the large, purple straw hat that had fallen over one eye. A gentleman of similar age in blue and green striped Bermuda shorts, a flowery Hawaiian shirt, black support socks, and white Keds righted the lady's hat and smiled at me.

Giggling, I just managed to avoid two tiny women with enormous mounds of curly jet black hair and matching sequin and rhinestone shirts. Pushing their sunglasses back up their noses in a unified movement, they stepped aside to let me pass, all the while looking me up and down. I snaked my way through the throng and into the shop.

I was in luck. The saleslady was free, and I stumbled past a large man with a toddler in his arms. The two of them seemed locked in an ill-fated struggle with a frozen yogurt cone. Just as I stepped up to the counter, they lost their struggle, and the cold, oozy mass landed on my foot. I stared at my chocolate-covered toes, wondering what to do as the kid gave out with an ear-splitting wail.

"God, how embarrassing!"

"There's a faucet out back on the dock, honey. You can wash your foot off out there. Lucky you're wearing those nylon sandals." The salesgirl looked sympathetic as she offered this advice.

"Gee thanks, but could I have four double A batteries, please?"

She responded with merciful speed. I grabbed my purchase and headed for the faucet. After a quick wash, I ambled back to our seats, trying to size up the crowd. Would I find some people my age on the island?

As I came around the other side of the building, I caught sight of J, and I hesitated. She was talking to a man, engrossed in conversation. The man looked up as I approached, and my aunt followed his gaze. She pointed the man toward the restrooms. He nodded and left.

"You know that guy, J?" I asked, trying to sound casual.

"No, he just wanted directions. C'mon, they're boarding the ferry now. Let's go."

We loaded up like two pack mules and headed for the boat. The coconut smell of tanning oil was everywhere. Sunglasses flashed in the sun like a field of sparkling mirrors. I felt a thrill of excitement, knowing that we were on our way.

Continuing in the pack-mule mode, we picked our way to the upper deck with none of the grace of those critters. Staking out our spot, I left Aunt Jill to protect our turf and headed for the rail.

Looking out across the Great South Bay, I could see Fire Island in the distance, a long stretch of dunes and scrub pines across the horizon. At the western end of the island was the black and white striped tower of Fire Island lighthouse, blinking away. Sailboats maneuvered across the dark blue waters of the bay in ballerina fashion, their sails puffed out by the wind like dancers' gauzy skirts.

"Annie, watch the bags, okay? I'm going to find the restroom."

Nodding, I ignored her warning about the bags. *What could happen to them on this ferry,* I thought. *It's just her line of work that makes her jumpy.*

Searching the lower deck for faces my own age, I mused about my next two weeks on the island. I was bound to meet people on the beach.

Out of the corner of my eye, I saw someone pause by our luggage. There go those city street smarts again. Looking up, my gaze fell upon a nondescript middle-aged man who was studying our stuff.

"Can I ..."

Before I could finish my question, he smiled, wheeled around quickly, and made for the lower deck. Leaning over the rail, I caught sight of his hurrying figure bounding down the gangplank.

With a hasty glance, I could see that the bags appeared undisturbed. On further examination, every zipper and flap was intact. I wondered where J was. Back at the rail, I leaned over, craning to see if she was on the lower deck.

Puzzled and amazed, I stared. There she was, talking to the same guy from the dock. *More directions?* I wondered, grabbing for the rail as the *Islander Queen* bumped through the piling and out of the slip. Despite the warm, gentle air around me, I felt an involuntary shiver.

J's work made me nervous sometimes. She was my closest friend. My parents were useless: Mom, with her roller-coaster ride through alcoholism recovery, and Dad, dedicated to his twice a week flights to the UK. I just didn't want anything to happen to her. Besides, my instincts were telling me that there was something funny about the guy who just took off and the one talking to J.

The man was tall and wore a black shirt and slacks in some silky material. His dark hair was slicked back with gel. He was a shiny man. All his surfaces were sleek. He was good looking in an adult sort of way that I associated with the foreign movies Aunt J seemed to favor.

My heart was thumping as I turned to look at the bags again. Craning my neck to see if J was on her way up the stairs, I could feel a cramping twinge of anxiety. J appeared at the top of the stairs, absorbed in some papers she was trying to remove from her purse, her face a study in tension. Seeing me watch her, she arranged her face into a smile.

"What's up?" She joined me at the rail.

"Uh, nothing. Just watching the scenery."

And scenery it was, capturing us for the next few minutes. The ferry plied its way out of the little harbor of Bay Shore, past the marina, its wake causing the boats that were tied up there to bob momentarily. They seemed to salute us as we passed. Once into the bay, we picked up speed, the breeze pulling our hair out of our faces. The salt air prickled my nose, and I wondered again about the two strange men.

Should I tell her? I wondered. The little angel-devil voice in my head argued briefly. Even if these guys meant something, J's not going to tell me, or she would have told me already, I decided. I felt left out, like some little kid.

"Look, Annie, you can see the little villages on the island now! Boy, it'll be good to spend the day on the beach tomorrow. I need some rest."

J's reassuring statement about the beach made me feel better. I pushed aside the urge to blurt out, "Who was that man? What's this all about?" This was going to be a great vacation, and I wasn't letting my overactive imagination ruin it.

"J, tell me about the house we're renting. You didn't fill me in on any details."

"Well, it's a fairly large house. It's one of the original ones built before the turn of the century. The man who owns it is John T. Egan, known to his friends as Doc. He's retired. Used to work for the CIA. He was a decoder."

"Geez, J! Don't you know anyone who has a normal job, like a teacher or a salesman?"

J laughed, warming to her subject. "He lives in a small wing on the house, and Annie, he has the neatest sailboat."

She reached out to hug me. "We're going to have the best time, Annie. I promise."

"Whoops, I think we're there." The engine noises quieted, and the ferry drifted like a swan toward the ferry slip. I had the weird feeling that the boat was standing still and that it was the island that was gliding toward us. The ferry dock had almost as many people on it as the ferry, but the dock people were dressed differently. Their attire was strictly T-shirts, shorts, and sandals. It was as if you only needed the brightly colored clothes to get onto the island. Once there, your feathers faded.

Besides their uniforms, each group of dock people had a red wagon like the ones we played with as kids. There were also rows and rows of red wagons hanging on racks on the dock.

How curious, I thought. And then it hit me. There are no cars here! You have to load all your stuff onto these wagons.

"Look at all those wagons," said J. "How cute!"

The faces on the people became clearer, and again I looked for faces around my age. There were a few likely candidates, and I wondered how I could meet them. My roving eyes came to rest on the top of a dark, shiny head of hair. The owner was bent over a wagon, unlocking it from the rack. His tan hands worked quickly, making the muscles in his back ripple across the shoulders of his white T-shirt in the most appealing way. As he straightened his body on a pair of long, tan, strong legs, he looked up at the ferry.

My legs started to tremble from standing on tiptoe and leaning over the rail. At least, I think that's why. I felt hot and realized I was blushing. *Boy, is he cool looking. How do I meet him?* I wondered.

"Absolutely gorgeous," escaped my lips.

"What?" J said as she poked me. "There's Doc!" she pointed.

"Oh!" Tearing my eyes away from Mr. Gorgeous, I saw what looked to me like Santa Claus after Weight Watchers. Full white beard, full head of white hair, rosy cheeks, and twinkling blue eyes gave character to a compact body. He was erect and tan in his white shirt, Levi's, and red suspenders. As I stared with pleasure, he turned to speak to the tall, dark boy I had noticed first. Together, they looked up at the ferry, shading their eyes to see the passengers. Aunt J waved furiously, blowing kisses at Doc when he spotted her. The boy smiled with a wide white grin flashing across his handsome sun-browned face.

My stomach flip-flopped as I realized my luck. I wasn't going to have to even try to meet this guy. He comes along with Doc.

"This is definitely going to be fun, huh, J."

J looked at me and just grinned.

Chapter 2
ENTER TY

FINE! JUST FINE! I THOUGHT as my panic-stricken mind cast about for a way to comb my hair and change my clothes before getting to the dock to meet the gorgeous one.

"Here, Annie, take these bags, will you? We're holding up progress here."

"How good could you look if you're disguised as a pack animal," I muttered.

J was already tossing the bags at me. I missed the first one, but J didn't miss me. The bag hit me squarely in the stomach, nearly knocking me down.

"Annie, land on the planet," she said with more than a hint of impatience. "I need help. Unless, of course, the transporter is working and we can beam the bags onto the dock."

I smiled sheepishly, smoothing my shorts and T-shirt, fluffing up my hair. I took a deep breath and started to pick up my share of the bags. J was already on her way to the line forming at the stairs. I hauled my load into position behind her with knees turned to Jell-o and a belly full of butterflies.

"Are you nervous about something?"

Damn J, I thought. *She's too perceptive.*

"No, I … Yes, I'm always nervous when I meet someone new, J. Aren't you?"

"Only when they're as cute as that kid with Doc, and they're my age." She winked at me. I could feel the red climb up my neck, hotter than any sunburn I might get here on the island. Mentally, I flipped through the various clever phrases I could use to make a startling impression on the boy on the dock.

"Hi, I'm Annie. You, Tarzan. Me, Jane." Uh, no, a little too strong, I think.

"Hello, I'm Annie Tillery. I'll be here on Fire Island for two weeks. Let's be best friends." Ugh, that's even worse. Maybe, I'll just smile.

We made our way down the stairs, one painfully slow step at a time, spilling out onto the dock. The crowd spread out like oil on water, stopped only by the barriers formed by the greeters with their wagons.

As I looked toward the spot where I had seen our host, the gorgeous one was gone. I scanned the dock desperately. *How could a whole adult-sized human being disappear*, I wondered. J came to a stop in front of Doc, and I plowed right into her.

"Doc, this is Annie, my niece." I reached out to shake his hand and, looking up, met his twinkling blue eyes.

"Pleased to meet you, young lady. Welcome to Fire Island. Just put your bags down there on the wagon."

He turned to J, and while he hugged her, I looked frantically around again. I must have imagined the boy I had seen. Perhaps he belonged with another group. I didn't think it would be cool to say, "Hey, where's the cute guy you were with, huh, Doc?"

J woke me out of my daze with that mixture of curiosity and annoyance in her voice.

"Oh, sorry. What is it?" I stumbled.

"We're ready to go on to the house now, Annie," said Doc. "Can you pull this wagon?" he asked as he skillfully led his wagon through the throng.

It took a minute to remember how to get the wagon to go in the direction I wanted to, but soon we were pulling away from the crowded dock area. We joined the parade on the boarded walkway that was the main thoroughfare in the tiny community called Point-O-Woods in which we found ourselves. I began to relax, look around, and let the ocean breeze cool the sweat on my body.

"Right this way," Doc called over his shoulder as he and J walked comfortably together, reviving their old friendship. While I wondered again about the disappearance of the boy I had seen, I noticed that Doc's footsteps sounded uneven. He had a slight limp. I made a mental note to ask J about that when we were alone.

The boardwalk opened onto a broad cement lane, where I could pull up next to J and Doc and walk beside them. On either side of us were homey little cottages, each with a tiny garden. The lane stretched before us to a clear horizon up ahead.

"Who lives in these houses?" I asked Doc.

"These are summer houses for the most part, Annie. People built them in the forties, when land became available. Before that, the land was owned by a corporation of rich businessmen who were against selling any of it. When we get up toward the beach and onto the boardwalk that runs along it, you'll see some of the big old fortresses those men built."

"Oh, look!" I gasped in a loud whisper. There, on the side of the house that we were passing, was a doe and her twin fawns, brazenly grazing on the shrubbery around the cottage.

"Aren't they afraid of people?" I asked.

"No, everyone here feeds them, but they carry a tick that causes Lyme disease," said Doc, "and no one knows what to do about them."

"Oh, they're so neat!" I exclaimed. And, with that, the three deer fled.

"I guess we can't take them home as pets," laughed J. "We couldn't very well walk them in Central Park," she joked.

Doc continued, "The house you'll be staying at is one of the original landowner's houses, Annie, and, I might add, one of the oldest on the Island. It even has a secret passage that was used during the twenties when liquor was smuggled onto Long Island from here."

"Can you show it to me?" My interest piqued, as I pictured an old house with creaking floors, gabled windows, and mysterious dark corridors.

"It doesn't go anywhere, since I boarded up the other entrance to keep people from breaking into the house in the winter."

"Oh, but I'd like to see it anyway!" I pleaded. We had turned east onto another boardwalk. Here the houses were further apart, larger, and older.

"These are called shingle houses for obvious reasons." Slowing his pace and switching the hand that pulled the wagon, Doc pointed, "And there is Windalee."

"What an odd name," J mused. "Is that your invention, Doc?"

"Yes and no. It used to be called 'The Wind is Alee,' which is a contradiction in nautical terms. Alee means sheltered from the wind, and the name is too long for my taste anyway. So, I shortened it to Windalee. It fits. The cottage gets the ocean breeze on one side, and the other faces the more sheltered bay."

"It's a great place!" I exclaimed, taking in the deep brown of the weathered shingles accented by white trim and shutters. Bright flowers cascaded out of window boxes, and beach plum roses twined themselves in the picket fence along the front walk. To someone who had lived in New York City all her life, this was truly a dream house.

As the wagons ground their way closer to the cottage, a loud, sharp yapping erupted. Awakened by the racket, two large sleek cats, one white with black markings, the other black with white markings, stretched, yawned, and rolled over on their backs as we approached.

Not able to resist a cat's furry underside, I bent to tickle them. *What a friendly place this is*, I thought, and said, "I'm really going to love it here," and continued tickling my furry hosts.

"Ooooh," I lost my balance as a set of strong little paws pounced on my crouched thighs. The yapping materialized into a coal black Scottish terrier, which scampered up to me and then away again excitedly.

"Easy does it, Merlin," a new voice admonished. As I watched for an opportunity to get to my feet between attacks, that long pair of brown legs came into view. I followed them up to the body and to the head they were attached to, and there he was, the boy from the ferry dock.

Merlin made one more attack and, catching me off balance, pushed me onto my butt. The boy extended his hand to me.

"Hi, I'm Ty. You must be Annie. Pleased to meet you."

For a moment, I sat there smiling up at him. I came to when I heard J clear her throat. "I'm pleased to meet me, too. I mean, you're pleased to meet me. I mean …" Feeling like a perfect fool, I finally resorted to, "Hi, I'm Annie. Thanks," as his strong grasp pulled me to my feet.

"Jill, this is my nephew, Ty Egan. He's helping me out here at Windalee this summer. He'll be going back to college in September, and we're trying to get the place shipshape for the winter."

J smiled and shook Ty's hand. I just smiled and thought that Fire Island must indeed be a paradise where dreams come true. In fact, my face was beginning to hurt from smiling.

With bags in hand, Ty and Doc took our stuff to our side of the house, where we were to stay. Doc grabbed a newspaper from the hall table as we entered and suggested, "Here's a copy of *Dan's Papers*. He's done a whole spread on Fire Island. You might want to read it." Excusing themselves, they went to see about dinner. As soon as we were alone, I flung myself at J and hugged her.

"This is going to be the best vacation, J, the best!"

She laughed and agreed.

"Let's get unpacked. I have to make a few phone calls before dinner, Annie. Also, Doc will keep us up late tonight. He's a great storyteller. And a great cook. If you get your stuff stowed quickly, you might want to wander up to the kitchen and ask Ty if he needs help." She smiled broadly as I blushed.

"What a great idea, J!"

I got down to the job at hand, passing quickly between the bathroom, the hall closet, and my dresser as the job demanded. I loved my room. It had four windows that met at the corner of the room. Through two of them I could just spy the ocean on the horizon beyond the dunes. Frilly white curtains billowed and collapsed as the gentle breeze caught them and let them go. All the woodwork in the room was a warm, natural wood tone, and the floor was the same wide plank wood. The rug and bedspread were snow white, and the walls were covered in a tiny blue-flowered print. It was peaceful and homey, yet the smell of the ocean and beach made it exciting for me.

As I finished unpacking, I could hear J on the phone. I wished she could just relax for the two weeks we were here. After a moment, I brushed that care aside, ready to explore. Skipping toward the door, I went out and soon realized that I was not in the same place as the door we entered originally. The house seemed to have as many doors and windows as it had shingles.

I came upon a wonderful little side porch that looked over the grassy dunes to the next house, a much smaller version of this one. *Could that have belonged to the estate of the original owner,* I wondered. I relaxed, feeling my muscles melt. The air smelled of ocean and tarred wood and bayberry. Then, intruding upon this beauty, came the odor of cigarette smoke. Instinctively, I looked for the source. My mother smoked. She also drank. The combination made me uneasy, and the smell brought back unpleasant memories.

As my eyes focused on the scene before me, I saw three people emerge from the other house. The cigarette belonged to a young guy, maybe twenty-five, who was gesturing emphatically to the two older men. I recognized one of them as the man J was talking to on the boat. He must be a guest on the island also, I surmised. The young man seemed to be gesturing toward Windalee.

Some sixth sense made me shrink into the shadows of the porch, but I continued to watch. All three of them looked at the house, and the mild ocean breeze raised unexplained goose bumps on my bare arms and legs. As the men turned to go back in the house, the "ferry" man's black shirt flipped open in the breeze to reveal a shoulder holster and a handgun. I couldn't make a mistake about that. I'd seen J's service revolver all too often.

The men disappeared, and I stood there staring at the ocean and hugging myself, chilled by the uncertainty of what these neighbors were all about. I shrugged, turning toward the path that led to the other side of the house. Living with my aunt the detective has made me too suspicious.

My spirits recovered as I met with the wonderful smell of frying potatoes and onions. Suddenly, I realized how hungry I was. The kitchen door opened and there was Ty. He smiled, waving me over. "Hey, we need some help in the kitchen. You came just in time."

He held the kitchen door open for me and followed me into a large, airy old-fashioned room fitted with the most modern kitchen equipment. I felt encouraged that our hosts seemed to be serious about preparing food, because I sure was serious about eating it.

Ty flashed his beautiful white grin. "How do you like the place?"

"When can I move in? Do you need a maid or a cook? So far, I love it. I can't wait to see the beaches."

"You won't be disappointed at all," he promised. "Look, Annie, I've got to help Doc with dinner. Could you tell your aunt that dinner is in half an hour, and if you have no other plans, Doc and I would like to take you sailing tomorrow. Okay?"

"Oh, super," I yelled and bounded out of the kitchen toward our rooms. Halfway down the path, I whirled around, "Do we have to dress for dinner?"

"Yeah," said Ty, who had been leaning against the door watching me, "We're very conservative on the island. Unlike some beach communities, we frown on nudity here." He put his hand over his mouth to hide his laughter, but his twinkling eyes couldn't keep his secret.

"Just what you're wearing is fine."

I tried a groan of protest, but it turned into a laugh, as I waved at him and headed for J's room. As I came in the door, I could still hear her on the phone. Her tone was serious. It made my ears perk up.

"Yes, I … contact with … No." A pause. "The … meeting … Bay Shore."

The screen door slipped out of my hand as I strained to listen. It slammed. J changed her tone immediately.

"Okay, will do. Yup, I'll keep in touch."

She hung up. The old familiar fear gripped me. She's on some case. It's probably dangerous. I didn't want that old worry now. I didn't want anything to ruin this vacation. I walked into her room. She met my troubled gaze for an instant.

I wanted to say, "If only you would tell me when you're on one of those cases, I wouldn't worry so much." But we'd been down this road before. I would get the "It's for your own safety" speech. She seemed to sense my concern, and she bounded off the bed, cheerfully neatening her room.

"What's for dinner, Annie, and when? I brought a basket of goodies from Balducci's for tonight. I am really looking forward to this. Go on and help Ty. I just have one more phone call to make."

I looked at her for a moment, wanting to ask whom she was calling. Dropping my hands to my sides, I gave up the idea and told her to be there in half an hour. As I headed back to the kitchen, I tried to tell myself that I was making a big deal out of a routine phone call, one of the hundreds I'd heard J make all my life. The lights were on in the kitchen, and dinner smelled great. I pushed aside the old bad feeling and thought about an evening with Ty.

Chapter 3
DINNER AT WINDALEE

I SET THE TABLE: DARK blue cloth and white china. Ty brought some puffy blue flowers he called hydrangea from the garden, and I put them in a vase he provided. The dining room, furnished in oaken antiques, had a well-worn, lived-in quality. Every available spot on the walls had a bracket for a hurricane lamp, and each was fitted with a stout candle.

It was still summertime light at 6 PM, but I could imagine how cozy and maybe even spooky this room could be when it got dark.

"Well, I think we could hire you, Annie. That's a beautiful job!"

Doc surveyed the table, looking for a place to put a tray of antipasto with cheese, sausage, olives, and eggplant thingies. "Your aunt remembered my passion for these nice Italian treats."

J poked her head into the room, looked around, and gave thumbs up. "Very nice! I'll get the wine."

Everyone appeared all at once, and we sat down to eat. As we made our way through the antipasto, the broiled local seafood, those heavenly fried potatoes with veggies, the conversation flowed easily. I became more comfortable with Ty and Doc, and J filled in the missing pieces since the last time she and Doc saw each other.

"I really admire you, Jill," Doc said soberly. "Crime in this area seems to be expanding into drugs and terror-related cases more and more. And, the criminals seem less and less worried about doing violence to the rest of us."

I thought of the men next door at the mention of violence, the sight of the one man's shoulder holster popping into my head.

"Doc," I piped up. "Who are those men next door?"

"They're seasonals," he said. "Renting the place for the summer. I keep a close eye on them. Don't like their looks. They avoid talking to me, and I think one of them has a gun. I'd like to check him out but can't seem to get any more information than what they put on the rental agreement, and that leads to dead-ends."

Well, I thought, *at least he knows about the gun.*

Ty looked serious. "They keep to themselves," but his frown told me he didn't like them much either.

"I have made some attempts to talk to them. I can catch a few words of conversation at times, when the wind blows in the right direction. I know it's not English, but I can't identify the language. My major at school is foreign studies. I'm interested in striking up conversations with people from other countries. I'm not sure if I want to specialize in South America or the Middle East. I made some good friends with my professors this year. One of them even held seminars in his home. I met his family, and I e-mail both him and his son. I've even make an attempt to communicate in their language.

"So anyway, I tried Spanish with our neighbors, but they just cut me dead. Unbelievably unfriendly for a beach community like this one."

After a pause, J picked up the conversation. "How's your leg, Doc? No more cane, huh?"

"Nope. The knee replacement worked. Don't have to worry about having my legs blown off anymore, so things should work out."

J responded to the look on my face, saying, "Doc'll never tell you this, but he took metal fragments from a bomb in his knee when he worked for the government. A terrorist attack on UN officials in Bosnia."

"Just part of the job. How about that peach pie now?" Doc shifted the subject deftly.

"This island must have some interesting stories," I ventured. "I mean, you even have a secret passageway." I was dying to see it.

"Oh, to be sure!" Doc responded with a wink. "From pirates, to freebooters, to shipwrecks, to bootleggers, drug runners. You name it! Being on the coast with a nice safe harbor makes this an ideal place for all manner of thuggery."

J put down her fork and stifled a yawn. "I'm sure we'll have plenty of time for stories in the next few days. I'm going to excuse myself. I'm beat. Good night everyone," she said brushing the top of my head with a kiss.

"I think that's a good idea," agreed Doc.

"I'll take care of the cleanup, Doc," Ty offered. "Will you help me clean up, Annie?"

You betcha, I thought. I would never be so enthusiastic about kitchen duty. "It's the least I can do," I replied, trying to keep the silly grin off my face.

Doc and J had gone to their respective rooms, and the dining room was very quiet. Ty cleared his throat and, looking a little nervous, asked, "Can you clear the table while I store the leftovers?"

"Sure can," said I, gleeful at the opportunity to continue our conversation and get to know Ty.

Chapter 4
FIRE ISLAND GHOST STORIES

THE NEXT MORNING BROUGHT A perfect sailing day. Over coffee I sighed, "Isn't he nice, J?" Of course, she knew I meant Ty.

"Yes, Annie. He's very nice. I was so glad when Doc told me he'd be here during our visit. He can really show you the island."

"How did you like Doc, Annie? He's a most interesting fellow. He'll be full of stories today, some that even I haven't heard. And how did you like dinner?"

Dinner had been something I would never forget. The best part for me, though, was spending the evening with Ty. He made me feel so comfortable. He seemed to really care about what I had to say. I helped him do the dishes after dinner, and we planned some things we could do together. Afterward, he showed me the boat he was building, a replica of the lifeboats used by the rescue teams that used to pick up survivors of shipwrecks from the terrible storms that ravaged Fire Island. He never said anything about his parents, and I was glad. I might feel that I'd have to talk about mine then, and I didn't want to. The less I thought about them, the better I liked it.

"Where are Ty's parents?" I asked on an impulse.

"Ty's lived with Doc for the last few years. His mother is dead, and his dad is in a mental hospital," she said quietly.

Our eyes met for a moment. I looked out the window, digesting the last piece of information. I felt an instant of closeness to Ty, and, of course, my thoughts flashed to my mother, her alcohol-ravaged face materializing in the TV screen of my memory.

"Did you have a nice time with Ty last night? You two talked for quite a while in the kitchen."

"Uh, yeah, I had a great time, J." I struggled to turn the channel on that mind-TV to another program. "What are you wearing on the boat?"

"A bathing suit and shorts, but I'm bringing sweats. It gets cold on the water toward evening."

The phone rang and I grabbed it, hoping it was Ty on the house phone. The voice on the other end made me tense up, as my heart skidded all the way down to my shoes. It was my father, good old Randall. I took a deep breath, closing my eyes tight, choking back the urge to say, "Dad, leave me alone. I came here to get away from you and Mom."

Instead came the well-practiced automatic response, "Hi, Dad, I'm fine. How are you?"

J looked up and motioned that she wanted to talk when I was done. "Dad, I'll call if I have anything new to talk about, okay? No, I'm not going to call Mom. I can't think of anything to say to her. Dad, please, we've been through this all before. Here's J. She wants to talk to you. I'll talk to you next week. Bye."

I handed the phone to J, who looked at me with that mixture of sadness and concern that made me feel guilty. I headed for my room.

"Damn, damn, damn!" I punched the pillows on the bed silently, and the tears slipped rebelliously between my tightly closed lids.

Why does he call me, I thought. *He's never home. If he were, maybe my mother wouldn't be wasting away in some rehab.* I wished he would make a clean break and go live overseas.

Clutching the pillow with all my strength, I stared through my tears at the calm ocean outside my window. Something warm brushed my leg. It was the black and white cat I'd seen yesterday. As I reached down to deliver a scratch to his head, he fell over in a heap, presenting his chubby white belly, expecting a tickle.

Losing myself in the warm silkiness of his belly and the hypnotic effect of his purring, I got myself together. *I'm not letting anything ruin this day,* I resolved. I promised myself that I wasn't going to deal with my parents' problems here on Fire Island. I made up my mind. *After J hangs up, I'm going to tell her to take all my father's future calls.* To him, I would be out and about.

I pushed myself off the floor and headed for J's room. As I rounded the corner in the hall, I heard a snatch of her conversation.

"Made contact yesterday."

That word again! It was hard not to try to listen in to J's telephone conversation. I wanted to know what was going on. I felt so out of control when I was in the dark. She might need help. How could I help her if she kept me in the dark?

I heard the receiver clunk into the cradle. Setting my jaw, I went into J's room. She looked up and, seeing my face, said, "Annie, don't let this phone call ruin your day, okay? There's no phone on Doc's boat."

"I don't want to talk to him if he calls again, J."

"He's your father, Annie. He cares about you. I wish you could try to talk to him."

Glaring at her, I managed, "We'll see. Right now, I'm going to count to ten and concentrate on having a good time."

A sharp yapping announced Merlin's arrival. Happily he ran in when I opened the screen door. He cocked his head to one side expectantly, as if to say, "Are you coming?" I scooped him up, giving him a hug, as he growled playfully and struggled to be free.

I rushed to dress and leave before the phone could ring again. Today was going to be an adventure, and I was going to be the main character if I had anything to say about it. Looking out into the yard, I called to J, "I'll meet you out front. I see Doc and Ty."

"Be right there, Annie."

The little marina at Point-O-Woods was crowded with gently bobbing boats. The breeze made a metallic symphony of sailboat halyards slapping against masts. The wind was just right for a day's sail.

Ty and I carried the cooler between us, our gear tucked into the knapsacks on our backs. J and Doc followed behind, J swathed in her hoodie and sweatpants and Doc in the same combination of clothes from the day before. We stopped in front of a dark blue thirty footer. Gold leaf carved into brightly varnished mahogany proclaimed the sloop's name to be *Star*, and she certainly looked it. The mast was enameled shiny white, the sail neatly furled in a yellow canvas cover. She had a teak deck, and the brass fittings flashed as the sunlight glanced off them. Doc beamed as I stared.

"Can I get on it?"

"You can certainly board her," he invited, correcting my landlubbers' ignorance of nautical terminology. Grinning, I shot back at him, "Do I have to walk the plank if I don't learn all the sailor words today?"

"Absolutely," he grinned back at me and laughed.

Timing my movements, I stepped over the low rope that ran around the deck of the sailboat. The low rope, I found out later, is called the lifeline. In rough seas, sailors tied themselves to it by a line so they wouldn't fall overboard. I made my way to the stern of the boat and stepped down into an area with seats, a tiller, and a bank of instruments.

"This is the cockpit," Ty offered in his casual soft-spoken manner. "If you like, I'll show you how everything works later."

"I'd like," I said as my eyes wandered over the maze of wires, ropes, and lines.

"It's not as confusing as it looks."

"When did you learn to sail?" I sat, bathed in the warm sun, listening to his soft voice, enjoying every minute.

"I don't remember when I didn't. I've always spent my summers here with Doc."

For a moment, I saw a flash of sadness in his eyes and then Ty grinned. Grabbing my hand and pulling me out of the cockpit, he said, "Let's help stow the gear, so we can be on our way."

In a few busy minutes, the food was put in the icebox, the sail cover was off and stowed, and all were on board. Ty deftly cast off the lines. At last, we were free of the mooring, motoring away from the dock.

Doc stood at the tiller, appraising the signs of the sea like a bloodhound picking up the scent of a rabbit.

"Don't like to sail away from the dock. Channel's narrow here, and you never know when the ferry'll be there," Doc muttered half to himself as he scanned the water for buoys that marked the way out of the little harbor. He squinted at the instruments and checked the wind vane on the top of the mast for wind direction.

When we were safely away from the channel, out in the bay, Ty hopped on the cabin roof and made ready to hoist the sails.

"Head'er up, Doc," he called.

Doc steered into the wind, and Ty yanked on the main halyard until the main sail was all the way up the mast. The breeze was stronger here in the bay, and the sail snapped and fluttered, its metal fittings making clanging noises as they slapped into the mast.

All of a sudden, the engine noise died, as Doc fell off the wind and cut the ignition. With a final crack, the sail filled, as Ty secured it with a line to a cleat. *Star* leaned to one side, as the wind grabbed the sail. The only sound was the hissing of sea foam, as it slid along the hull.

I couldn't take my eyes off the sail. Gaily colored streamers fluttered on the sail.

Following my gaze, Ty said, "Those are called telltales. They let you know how the air is moving over the sail, so you can adjust it to get the maximum out of the wind."

Staring at the huge white sail, all I could manage was, "Oh."

"Ty, hoist the genny. We'll have a good ride with it today."

With that, Ty went all the way to the bow, disappearing on the other side of the main sail. There was a metallic scrapping noise, and up came another sail along the big cable that ran from the bow to the top of the mast. Doc sheeted this sail in, and the boat dug into the water a little more, picking up speed.

J took a seat on the upside of the cockpit and braced her legs on the opposite seat.

"This is heaven!" she sighed and smiled at Doc.

"I think we'll head for Smith's Point today. That'll give us good run back." With that, Doc checked his compass and knot meter. He tied the tiller in place and disappeared into the cabin.

Ty caught my doubtful look and said, "That's our autopilot."

Doc reemerged with iced tea and soda for all, and we spent the next few minutes absorbing the wonder of sailing.

From this vantage point, Fire Island passed by us on one side, Long Island on the other.

"Doc, how did Fire Island get its name?"

"That's a good question, Annie. There are quite a few theories. Long Island itself was a very important trade center, even from colonial times. There were whaling ports here as important as any in the world. As you can see, this bay makes the south shore of Long Island a very desirable safe port. The problem was to get past Fire Island and into the bay itself."

"That's right. I heard that on the news." I piped in. "Fire Island is always shifting."

"We get some bad storms here, and that shifts the sand in the inlets," Ty added.

J roused herself and observed, "Today, they only worry about summer homes falling into the drink."

"Well, anyway, the inlets became very important. In order to guide ships through the inlets and into the bay, the colonials built big bonfires at openings into the bay. The British weren't building lighthouses here, and the colonials couldn't do it without asking permission. Although this was a prosperous colony, so much money was paid to the British by the colonists that they couldn't have afforded it anyway."

"Didn't that cause a lot of shipwrecks, though?" asked Ty. "Because many ships' captains didn't know which side of the fire to come through on."

"Not as many as when the pirates took over," added Doc.

"Pirates? There were actually pirates on Fire Island?" I was astonished.

"More than anywhere on the East Coast. Remember, there was a lot of shipping in these waters," Doc continued as he checked the sails.

"And shipwrecks," came a muffled J from under her sun visor.

"Yes, the shipwrecks go back to the 1600s. Divers come from all over the country to explore them." Ty brushed hair from his eyes and pointed toward a break in the land on the horizon. "That's the inlet."

"It doesn't look treacherous," I remarked. Standing to get a better view, I cracked my head against the boom, seeing stars for a moment.

"Ouch," I rubbed my head, and to my surprise, everyone was laughing.

"Oh, sorry," giggled J.

Ty snorted into his cupped hand, as he descended into the cabin.

"Don't mind them, Annie," smiled Doc. "Everybody does that before they get used to a sailboat. Even some who are used to it still do it on occasion. It looks so damn funny, though," he trailed off in a gale of laughter.

Trying to get the attention off myself, I said, "Doc, why is the inlet so dangerous? I don't see any rocks. The water is very calm here."

"That's just it, Annie. Rocks don't shift, but sand does. The deepest part of the inlet shifts around according to the weather. And, don't let the calm waters deceive you. These are quiet weather conditions. All you need do here is reverse the wind direction, and you would see large combers rolling toward shore. You know, those are the waves the surfers love."

Ty emerged from the cabin with cold drinks and a plate full of sandwiches. They smelled delicious, and all of a sudden, I was starving. J sat up from her doze, instantly awake, and we all dove into the food.

By this time, we had cleared the inlet, and Doc turned *Star* in an easterly direction to run along the shore of Fire Island. While he was doing that, some strange domestic urge took me over, and I rose to clear the lunch debris. A strong but gentle hand pulled me back into my seat, as the boom whizzed by again over my head. The hand lingered a moment, and I squeezed back, a curious thrill running down my legs.

"You have to watch out for that thing, Annie."

I tilted my head up and looked into that warm grin just inches away from my face. Warmth flooded through me, and I laughed, very conscious of his nearness.

"I see that. Teach me to sail, and maybe I'll learn to avoid the boom."

Ty looked inquiringly at Doc, who said, "Go ahead, my legs are tired anyway."

For the next half hour, Ty explained the physics of sailing, all the while standing close to me and guiding my hand on the tiller. Wanting to impress him, but wanting more just to feel the thrill of catching the wind and propelling the boat through the sparkling water, I put my mind to being my best student-self.

Soon, I got the hang of it and was able to look at the shore passing on our port side, the endless stretch of white beach dotted with its colorful inhabitants. Each beach house peered into the sea from mirrorlike windows, signaling passing ships with vibrantly hued flags, pennants, and wind socks.

"Doc, with all these shipwrecks, there must be some interesting folklore around. You know, local superstitions, legends, and the like," inquired J, giving up her snooze to keep Doc company as Ty and his student kept the ship on course.

"What about ghost stories?" I added, tightening the main. "I collect ghost stories. I started when I was doing a sixth-grade project and never stopped."

"In the early 1800s, many settlers came to Long Island," Doc launched into his story. "First the men came to establish a home site and then they sent for the women and children.

"Usually, the ships avoided coming to Long Island between August and November because of the hurricane season, but this one particular ship was delayed in Jamaica and arrived off the coast just in time for a tropical storm. According to the records kept by the church in Bay Shore that cared for the survivors, it wasn't a full-blown hurricane but a bad storm with a full gale."

Doc had our full attention now, as we imagined the wooden sailing ship tossed in a sea turned treacherous by tropical winds.

"Her name was the *Hebrides*, and her cargo was twenty-four women and sixteen children, with a crew of eight. The good fortune of the twelve survivors was that the boat broke up on a sandbar similar to the one we're passing right now. See it over there, the strip of light green water over there.

"The story goes that the women lashed their small child to themselves with their shawls before they jumped overboard to swim ashore. This action proved to be fatal for some of the children. They couldn't struggle to the surface to breathe, and most of the mothers were not swimmers anyway. They were at the mercy of the waves."

I felt tears well in my eyes as I pictured this horrible struggle. All eyes were on Doc.

"Many women who made it to shore arrived with drowned babies, the joy of their own survival dashed by the guilt and grief of losing their babies in such a tragic way."

"Did all the children die?" I asked, gulping back a lump in my throat. A vision of my own mother popped, uninvited, into my head. With an involuntary shudder, I blew the thought right out of my head to wherever it had come from.

"No. Some could be revived, and this drove one woman in particular to wander up and down the beach, trying to find someone who could revive her baby.

"When they saw that her child was dead, the good people from Bay Shore tried to comfort her. She was suffering from exposure and had a serious wound on her arm, but no one could calm her, nor did they have time to stop their rescue work for her. She wandered the beach, her baby clutched to her, until she collapsed and died herself. Her grave is in the old cemetery in Bay Shore."

"Oh, how sad," murmured J.

Ty had taken over the tiller. I wiped a tear as Doc continued.

"Soon after, people claimed to see her frantically walking the beach on stormy nights. Even today, the Madonna Ghost, as she is called, is sighted by people on occasion. Once, a team of folks from one of the local colleges came to study what they called a paranormal event. They scared the ghost away for months."

"What a great story, Doc! Have you seen her yourself?" asked J.

"Don't believe in ghost stories myself, Jill. But some on the island swear to have sighted her."

We sailed on into the afternoon, warmed by the sun. I couldn't get Doc's ghost story out of my head.

"It's time to head back, I think. Ready to come about?" he called.

Ty shifted to the other side of the cockpit. I decided to follow him just as Doc turned the boat into the wind. The boom came swinging around to the lee side of the boat, and this time I ducked before Ty grabbed me. My hat went flying, and as I watched it bob away on the waves, I muttered, "I'll get the hang of this yet."

J retired to the cabin, and Doc busied himself with the task of adjusting the sails.

"I've seen her," Ty said quietly, "and I know someone on the island who's seen her also."

At first, I thought, *Who? Seen who?* As the light dawned, I looked up at him, feeling a thrill of excitement.

"You're kidding. This is a joke, right?"

I could see by his face that it wasn't a joke.

"No joke. But, if you don't believe me, we'll just skip it, okay? I don't talk about it with Doc. He thinks it's crazy stuff."

"Could I see the ghost?" I felt silly asking, but when I looked up at Ty again, the thrill of excitement quivered once more.

"Tomorrow night." He looked at me with a gleam of excitement in his eyes. "The next couple of nights might be the time to watch for her. There's no moon."

"Tomorrow night, then." I felt a chill as a cottony cloud passed in front of the sun.

The sky brightened as it had dimmed. Our plans to find the Madonna Ghost tomorrow night gave me a sense of closeness with Ty. I liked the feeling. I wanted to touch him in some way, to hold his hand or lean on his muscular brown arm. The feeling was so intense that I looked around to see if anyone else in the boat could see the waves of energy pulsating from me to Ty.

At that moment Ty turned to me, not smiling, just looking at me. I didn't know what the look said exactly, but I felt even more drawn to him.

"Time to drop the sails, Ty," called Doc.

The mood shattered like ice in a windstorm. Ty was up on deck in a jiffy. Soon, the sails were down and stowed.

"Thanks for a great day, Doc." J yawned with contentment. "I'm so relaxed, you can just throw a blanket on me here in the boat. I'll sleep like a pup."

Relaxed was the last word I would use to describe my mood. I wanted to keep on sailing. I wanted to become an expert sailor. Tonight! But most of all, I didn't want to leave Ty. I had a million questions that I wanted to ask him. I wanted to find out all about him. This longing made me tingly in a way I never felt before.

While I had been lost in my daydreams, we had arrived back in the marina. Doc and Ty secured the boat, while J and I gathered our gear to return to Windalee. By the time we walked back to the house, it was dark. The beach grass rustled mysterious whispers in the cool breeze, while crickets chirped with all their might.

"C'mon, Annie," said J. "We've had a long day."

Reluctantly, I said good night to Ty and Doc.

"Don't forget our tour of the beaches tomorrow, skipper." Ty winked at me. "You did a great job sailing the boat," he added as he backed away from me, almost falling over Merlin, who was in the process of sniffing out where his people had been.

"Thanks. Bye," I answered, feeling abandoned. I stood, rooted to the ground, watching Ty fade into the gloom of the yard. J tugged at me gently.

"Annie, you'll see him tomorrow. Don't worry. Doc locks him in his room at night, so nobody can kidnap him. Okay?" J smiled and shook her head as I followed her inside, giggling at the ridiculous picture she had just painted.

Now, I was very sleepy. I slipped into bed, not even able to brush my teeth, and soon was dreaming about the beach on the other side of the dunes. Somewhere in the dream, Ty and the Madonna Ghost were playing volleyball on the beach.

Chapter 5
ALICE IN "WONDERLAND"

"WELL, HELLO, SLEEPYHEAD," CAME A muffled greeting from Ty, who was buried under a mound of nylon sail. At first I thought he was picking at the sail, but as I approached, I could see that he was sewing. "Almost done," he announced. "Ready for a beach tour?"

"You bet! I can't wait to ride those waves. Can I help you fold that sail? Or whatever it is that you do with it." It was another beautiful day, clear blue sky with just a touch of haze coming off the water.

"Just help me stuff it back into the bag, and we can go." Ty offered the bag to me and began cramming the sail into it. He tossed it into a utility shed, grabbed my hand, and off we went over the dunes and onto the beach.

The sea was a lovely, dark greenish blue. Its color lightened to the glassy sheen of an old Coke bottle where the breakers curled onto the shore. White sand with amethyst swirls lay like a soft, undulating carpet between us and the surf line. The air hissed with a sea that coolly tickled our skin with its spray.

"What's that purple stuff in the sand?" I asked, drinking in the loveliness of the day.

"Clamshells. The varieties of clams we have here have an inner coating that's purple. The waves pulverize them into fine grains, and the surf makes those designs in the sand."

"Neat," I murmured, feeling the urge to jump into the water. As if he had read my mind, Ty started to peel off his T-shirt. I did the same, and hand in hand, we plunged through the surf to the gentle swells beyond.

The water delivered an icy shock at first that eased to refreshing coolness as we bobbed in the swells. Salt stung my eyes, and sun glinted off the water's changing surfaces in blinding flashes. I swam for a short distance, parallel to the shore, turning on my back to float. Ty reached out and grabbed my hand. We floated together, listening to and feeling the sea around us.

"How did a city kid like you learn to swim so well?" he challenged.

"My school has a swim team. We use the pool at the N.Y. Athletic Club. Everyone at school has to join a team, and I'm a zero at ball sports. I decided it was the swim team for me." I thought how different this was from the N.Y.A.C. pool.

"I can't imagine what it's like to grow up in a big city with no ocean and no wide-open spaces," mused Ty.

"It's all I ever knew," I responded, feeling the need to defend my life. "I see it as a great big jungle gym, or maze, that you need to get to know. Early on, you learn where not to go. And, what is safe."

"How's that?" asked Ty paddling us closer to shore as we drifted along.

"Usually from parents and teachers. Sometimes, from experience." I remembered my childhood fear of cars pulling up close to me at the curb. Once, a woman tried to pull me into her car. I got her to let go by scaring her with my cap pistol.

"There's a surprise around every corner, and so much to do. You'd be surprised at how many cool things there are to do in New York City."

"You make it sound interesting," said Ty. "I'd like to see it."

"J and I can show you a good time in the big city, Ty. Come and visit us." I winked, inadvertently squeezing his hand. He squeezed back.

"Hey, I see Alice," exclaimed Ty. "She's the one who's seen our ghost. Let's go talk to her." With that, we dove back through the surf. Soon, we were standing on the beach, drying off with our T-shirts.

Alice was about five hundred yards down the beach, a figure swathed in vivid colors, face shadowed by a big hat. Two large dogs making whoofing noises bounded alternately into the surf and around her legs.

"Don't be surprised by anything Alice says," warned Ty. "She is quite the eccentric. Good lady, but she can be out there sometimes."

Alice glided into view. At closer inspection, she was very tall and elegant. She was also much older than I had guessed. Her skin was creased by a myriad of tiny wrinkles, and it was nut brown. Her hair wound around the crown of her head in a dark, silvery braid. She wore a halter and long beach skirt of azure, lavender, and hot pink. She had layers of bracelets and chains. There was a ring on every finger, and a huge crystal dangled from one of her neck chains.

"Alice DeLea, this is Anne Tillery. She and her aunt are staying with Doc and me for a couple of weeks." Alice took the hand I offered and held it firmly, gazing directly into my eyes. She held this pose for a moment and then her face crinkled up into a smile.

"You have a beautiful, open face, Anne. Easy to read your character. Just like Ty," she observed. I didn't know what to say to this embarrassing, first-meeting analysis. Ty said not to be surprised. I just managed, "I prefer Annie to Anne, please."

"Annie it is, then. How do you find Fire Island so far?"

"It's been a great change for me from the city. I love the beauty of it, and yesterday, I heard there's some mystery to it as well." I glanced up at her to see her reaction.

She had been absently scratching the ears of one of the dogs. She looked at me, eyes narrowed. She seemed to be trying to judge my meaning.

"I told her about our ghost, Alice," said Ty. "She'd like to take a look at her."

"What are your experiences with ghosts, my dear?" Alice became all business. Her question threw me for a loop. What was this, a job interview?

"Uh, none. I collect ghost stories," I added lamely. "I do think they're real, though." I tried to sound convincing. She continued to gaze at me for a moment longer.

"I tell you what," she said, rousing herself from the long gaze. "Ty and Annie, come over to my place. We'll talk some more about this where we can be more comfortable."

I hadn't noticed until now that the sun had grown very hot. I could feel my shoulders prickling with sunburn. I pressed a finger into my shoulder and noticed the white dot it left that was the telltale sign of too much sun.

"Yeah, the sun is strong," observed Ty, tossing me a shirt. "Time to get out of it." Off we went, trudging through the soft sand, savoring every puff of cooling breeze that came along.

Alice's house was modern, lots of decking and huge windows. She led us up the path to a gate that announced this house to be called Glass House. Once inside, we climbed a circular stairway into a cavernous living room, floor to ceiling windows on three sides, giving an unparalleled view of the ocean. There were wind chimes hanging everywhere, tinkling melodically in the breeze from the open sections of window. A dream catcher hung in every open section of glass, and sun catchers liberally sprinkled the stationary sections of glass, representing every form of sea life imaginable. The name Glass House fit. Soft music of the meditation variety added a soothing backdrop.

"You two sit down and make yourselves comfortable, while I get us some refreshments." Alice left us alone. We sat on opposite sides of the room, and Ty winked at me.

"Quite an unusual place, is it not?" He smiled.

"I like it. It's airy, and all these beautiful things make it seem alive." The place gave me a good feeling, peaceful, yet alert to the sensations it evoked in me.

"J and I went to Sante Fe on our last vacation. We visited a Hopi Indian craft shop, and they were selling those dream catchers." I gestured toward the web-like objects in the windows. "They're supposed to catch your bad dreams as they come into your home and let the good ones in. Nice idea!"

"Alice gave me one for my room," said Ty, intently rubbing one of the dogs behind the ear. "Seems to work," he grinned. "Haven't had a bad dream in a while."

Alice returned with iced tea, fruit, and granola cookies. We wolfed down everything she brought and were working on the refill, while Alice rummaged around at a large, antique, roll top desk. She returned with a manila envelope.

"There is a great deal of history here on the island. Someday I'm going to write a book." Alice rummaged around some more. "Shipwrecks, lighthouses, life-saving services, bootlegging, drug running, terrorism, even kidnapping." She was sounding like Doc.

"What's bootlegging?" I asked.

"Oh, back in the 1920s, sale of alcoholic beverages was illegal, and so liquor from Europe was smuggled in. This was a huge business, because people paid a high price for that stuff, mainly because it wouldn't kill you like the stuff they made in secret factories here. It was made from all kinds of poisonous chemicals like wood alcohol, and it became known as bootlegging. What folks won't do for money.

"Where is that article?" Alice continued her search and to give us a history lesson.

"Did you know that during World War II, heads of state even met on naval ships to plan strategy off shore?

"Ah! Here it is!" Alice stood up. "Do you believe me when I say that I have seen this ghost?" Her eyes seemed to bore into my brain, looking for my answer.

"Uh, I guess so. That's why I'm here. But, do I believe beyond a shadow of a doubt? I don't know, Ms. DeLea. I don't have any experience with ghosts. The fact that both Ty and you have seen her makes it seem more real. And, I sure would like to see her."

"Why?" she challenged.

"Why?" I repeated, trying to give her some kind of an intelligent answer. "Ghosts are fascinating stuff. If they do exist, what if you could talk to them? Imagine the great things they could tell you."

"Some are evil," she shot at me.

"But not the Madonna Ghost. Is she?" This was making me very uneasy.

Ty sensed my discomfort and explained, "Alice takes the spirit world very seriously."

"What would you do with the experience of seeing a ghost?" Alice continued with her interrogation.

"I don't know. I haven't thought it through. I … I think it might change my view of ghosts somehow. I can't answer your questions until

I see one. Can I?" I was beginning to think that this was a bad idea. I was about to make a polite exit when Alice, coming to some decision, responded.

"I like your being honest with me, Annie." With this, she opened the manila envelope. Inside were neatly snipped newspaper clippings of a considerable age. There were photocopies and copies of old films called microfiche as well. That was the way data used to be stored.

"I've been researching some about our ghost. In fact, I know the archivist at the Long Island Historical Society. He's helped me to accumulate a lot of material on M. G., as I like to call our sad lady."

That was eerie, I thought. *She calls her ghost by initials, and I do the same with my aunt.*

"Doc told us about her yesterday," I offered. "At least she was a real person."

Alice nodded. "I have been seeing her regularly for the last two years. At first, I thought the figure that I was seeing was a late-night bather. I go out to the dunes to meditate at night. The sound of the surf and the vision of the stars on moonless nights help me to shut out the world."

"What made you think that the bather was really a ghost?" I asked, thinking the bather more likely than the ghost.

"I did think it was a bather. However, one night I called out to her to warn her of a strong undertow. She wouldn't answer me, and I hurried after her. Just as I was almost upon her, she disappeared."

"How did you know it was a her?" I pressed. "What did the ghost look like?" I tried to imagine a ghost. All I could come up with was some transparent filmy form.

"I thought it was a her because of the long robe the figure was wearing and the way it walked. She appeared like a real person, except there was a faint glow all over her. I didn't know what to make of that."

"She always looked like that to me," added Ty. "And she always disappears in the same place. It's very curious." Ty looked up to meet Alice's gaze, as they both pondered this mystery.

"Did you see the ghost together the first time?" I asked.

"No. Ty came across me one day, rooting around where I had seen her disappear. He asked me what I was doing. Something about the way he looked when he asked me made me tell him the truth."

"When I told Alice about my experience with the so-called bather, we were convinced that we had a real ghost," added Ty. "The next night we waited for her together."

"We've seen her while we're together three times now. It's hard for us not to think that she's authentic." Alice said this with conviction.

"Do you try to talk to her?" I asked.

"Oh. Of course! She just glides on by with no response. I don't want to go right up to her. That would be dangerous for both me and the ghost." Alice's knowledge of ghosts fascinated me. I sat on the edge of my chair, waiting for the next revelation.

Alice continued, "To my knowledge, there hasn't been a Madonna Ghost sighting since those parapsychologists came to study her some years back. The locals can be quoted as saying, 'Them college folks were enough to scare the devil away with all their paraphernalia.'"

"So then, you and Ty are the only ones to have seen her since?" I calculated quickly in my head. "That's forty years ago." I looked at them both.

"No one has come forward to admit seeing her," Ty responded.

"Maybe they don't think what they're seeing is a ghost," I said. "How do you know that this is a ghost?"

"Oh. She's a ghost, all right!" declared Alice. "If you saw her, you'd know that yourself." Alice returned to the contents of the envelope on her lap.

"I want you to read this account of an M. G. sighting from the twenties. It gives a good description of her."

I scanned through the article dated July 12, 1927, from the *Babylon Beacon*, until I got to the eyewitness account.

Garth Verity, a Fire Island rescue team member was on patrol on the night of July 10, when he made what he claims is a ghost sighting. Mr. Verity gave the following description of the apparition known to Fire Islanders as the Madonna Ghost.

"She came right out of the surf. Startled me half to death. I ran towards her, thinking that she must have fallen from a boat. No one was swimming in the area to my knowledge. It was very rough surf that night. I knew she wasn't a swimmer either, because she was wearing a long dress, and she was clutching a bundle. I don't know how she made it through the surf in that get-up. But what was most curious was this funny kind of light that seemed to make her glow.

Anyway, I heard crying, and I got really upset. I thought the bundle must be a child. As I got up to her, she just disappeared. I searched everywhere, even knocking on people's doors. No one ever saw her. It was the strangest thing that ever happened to me on the beach."

The article went on to say that many strange occurrences had been happening since the passage of Prohibition. As soon as the sale of alcoholic beverages became illegal in the United States, there was a lot of smuggling from offshore boats onto Fire Island.

I looked up from the paper, and Alice, who had been watching me intently, said, "That is a perfect description of what I saw."

At that point, Ty said emphatically, "Not only that, but Alice and I have noticed that there is another weird coincidence. Whenever we see M. G. it's always a new moon, when the amount of natural light is the least."

"Yes," Alice interrupted. "And on July 10, there was a new moon! I looked it up in the almanac."

"Annie," Ty said quietly, touching my knee, "There's a new moon tonight." I looked from Ty to Alice. The thrill of expectation vibrated through all three of us.

"Let's meet in the dunes, then. At midnight," said Alice, closing the envelope on her lap. "You can judge for yourself, Annie. Is she a ghost or not?"

Chapter 6
The Neighbors

"You don't have to do this if you don't want to, Annie, if this scares you or anything." Ty looked anxious as we walked away from Alice's house.

"I'm not scared, exactly," I said, trying to put a name to my feelings. "I just didn't think this was going to be so serious. I thought it would be fun to see a ghost. How did you feel about it, Ty? Was it fun? Or scary? Or what?"

"It was confusing. I didn't know it was a ghost at first. Alice was the one who opened that possibility for me."

"And you believed her," I said half to myself. Ty was silent. At last I decided, "I guess I do have to see for myself." I looked at Ty and offered my hand. "Let's shake on it, then. I do want to see M. G."

We shook hands solemnly and then laughed. The bright sun and the beach would not let us be serious for too long.

"I have to run some errands for Doc." Ty gazed at the summer-perfect horizon, seeming as reluctant as I to see this day come to an end.

"And I want to see what J is up to," I added. A sobering thought struck me. "I wonder how J is going to feel about my doing a midnight ghost watch."

"Probably about the same as Doc. He humors me but doesn't seem to put too much stock in the whole idea of ghosts."

"Geez. What if she wants to come with us?" I began to giggle as I pictured J, the ultimate logical detective, dealing with our ghost. The giggles turned into full gales of laughter. Ty looked at me with a mixture of curiosity and amusement.

"What is so funny?" he finally asked.

As I caught my breath, I managed, "I was just picturing J trying to interrogate the ghost. The ghost ignores her. She tries to arrest the ghost. How do you Mirandize a ghost? The ghost disappears. She puts out an APB on M. G."

Ty smiled at my picture. "She and Doc make a good pair. Just too much logic and not enough romance."

"I don't know about that," I mused. "I'd like to think there's a lot of fire there. Just look at the exciting lives they've lived."

Finally, with a jaunty wave that gave my heart a neat little lurch, Ty headed down the beach for the marina, leaving me to return to Windalee on the boardwalk. It was a lot faster than walking on the beach. Soon I began to recognize the houses near Windalee.

What would J's reaction be to my ghost watch? I wondered as I quickly covered the distance. I thought about my father for some reason, trying to imagine what his reaction might be. He probably wouldn't let me go. Too dangerous. Too late at night. Too …

"Ouch!" I yelled. I was so lost in my speculations that I didn't notice the bicycle that was lying partway onto the boardwalk. Moaning softly and clutching my ankle, I sat on the wooden planks, blinking back tears of pain. As the pain eased, I assessed the damage. I had to take off my T-shirt and rip off a piece to stop the bleeding from the cut. There was a big bruise blossoming as well.

Next, I surveyed the bike. I had fallen onto the front wheel and bent several spokes. Damn, I thought. Now I have to tell the people in the house that I broke their bike. I'd like to tell them how stupid they are for leaving it lying across the walk. I got up, testing my ankle. It seemed okay. Painful, but I was walking in a passable manner. I limped past the bike and made my way toward the door to explain what happened. The people were obviously home, since I could see the inside of the house through the screen door.

To my surprise, this was the neighbors' house, the one I had seen the first night, across the dunes from Windalee. I was on the other side of it. I paused on the front porch, wondering whether to drag the bike off the path. Voices rose from inside the house. I listened, attempting to judge what kind of people I'd have to face. I conjured up the faces of the men I had seen that first night. I could hear two men arguing. A third voice sounded like a referee.

"I *must* know that information," said one voice.

"You'll be told what you need to know," came the answer.

"You two had better cool it," piped in Number Three.

Something crashed to the floor. I turned to leave the porch. This didn't seem the right time to tell them about the bike. I could come back later.

"We need to know who this contact is. I don't like it that these guys …"

The conversation trailed off, but I had already stopped dead in my tracks at that word again. "Contact," there it was again. The hairs on my sunburned back stood up.

"Hey! Who are you? What are you doing here?"

One of the men had come around from the back of the house. Startled, I nearly jumped out of my skin. I blurted out, "I broke your bike. Some dope left it out on the walkway, and I tripped on it. I was just trying to let someone know."

The younger man was advancing toward me. I kept on backing up. Initially, he startled me. Now, he was frightening me. He was big and dark, his scowl making him look like an advancing thunderhead. He was angry.

I backed into the porch railing, which hurt. It also reminded me that this guy had me trapped. Panic turned my knees to rubber, and instinct took over. I lunged at him, screaming at the top of my lungs, "Get out of my way. You can't talk to me that way. I'll have you arrested for endangering a minor."

Those were the first things I could think of. They worked. Rushing past a very astonished man, I flung over my shoulder, "Don't leave your stupid bike in the path, you bully. I almost broke my leg. I'm going to send you the doctor's bill."

I just kept on going, shaking all over. My leg hurt. My heart was pounding out of my chest, and I was crying like a baby when I reached Windalee. Luckily, no one was there to witness this. I tried to compose myself, wetting down my leg at the outside hose. Making myself as presentable as possible, I entered the house, heading for J's room.

The house was quiet. J's room was empty. There was a note on her bed, the room as neat as a pin. I read the note, my heart skidding through my gut and into my feet.

> *Dear Annie,*
> *So sorry. I was called back to the city. Doc said you can sleep in the spare room at his house if you're not comfortable here. Should be back in a few days. I love you, little Annie.*
> *J*
> *P.S. Your dad called. Call him back, please.*

I sat on the bed, tears flooding out with no attempt on my part to check them. Disappointment smothered me. I had so wanted J to be here. Just once, I wanted her job to go away. Right now, I needed her here to listen to my story about the neighbors. I could always call Lt. Red. He might be able to put me in touch with J. But I knew better. She would be on assignment, with no way to speak to her directly. This was hardly an emergency.

And on top of everything else, I had to call Dad. I went into the bathroom to take a cool shower, hoping it would help to clear up my thinking. The phone rang. *Oh God. Now what?* I thought.

"Hello. Oh, hi Dad." I suppressed the urge to just hang up.

"Didn't you get my message, Annie?" came the familiar voice on the other end.

"I just got in Dad. I'm supposed to be having fun in the sun here, not sitting by the phone," I snapped back.

"Mom is doing much better, and she's been asking for you."

Wow, she remembers who I am. What a bonus! I thought. "I'm glad to hear that, Dad. What are you calling me for?"

"Annie, because I love you, and I'm your father. I'm tired of apologizing to you for my job, for Mom. Those things just are. If you could come to accept them, maybe you could come to cope with them in some better way. I don't like being treated like trash every time I call."

I bit my lip, hearing the hurt in his voice. I could understand hurt. "Not having your parent there when you need them, Dad, makes me feel like trash, too," I answered quietly.

"Annie, that's why I'm on the phone, I'm trying to be there as much as I can."

"Where are you now, Dad?"

"I'm at Kennedy. I'm taking Delta 609 at 5 PM. I wanted to make sure you're okay before I leave."

I could feel the tears breaking through the iron gate of my will to keep them back. I wanted to tell him how frightened I had been, how my leg hurt, how stupid I felt. J was gone. He was going. The old loneliness was like a vacuum, sucking out all my strength. "Well, Dad, have a good trip, and I'll speak to you when you come home," I managed, almost choking on the word "home."

"Will you call Mom?"

"No, Dad. Not yet. I can't. And, that's that."

"Okay, Annie," came the resigned sigh on the other end. "I love you and take care."

"Yes. Good-bye, Dad." I hung up and sat there sobbing, trying not to wish both my parents dead, just missing.

The shower washed away some of the pain along with the salt and the sand. I dressed and blew out my hair. It was time to hunt out Doc or Ty to see if I could get some first-aid stuff for my leg.

As if I had summoned him, a voice called out, "Hey! Can I come in?"

"I've got some fresh lemonade," came a cheerful, much-welcomed Ty.

My spirits rose at the sight of him, freshly showered and dressed in clean clothes. He started to put the jug of lemonade down on the table but stopped in midair.

"What happened to you, Annie?" he demanded, looking me up and down. Concern filled his face, as his eyes searched mine. He didn't miss the red, swollen eyes.

"I fell over a bike someone left on the boardwalk. I got a pretty good gash, and ..." I stopped trying to gain control of the tears. "I'm sorry. I'm upset. It's not just the leg. When I tried to tell the people in the house that I broke the bike when I fell over it, one of the men got really nasty."

"Nasty, how?" Ty wanted to know.

"He started to come at me. I was on the porch, and he came from around the back. I managed to run past him. It's the house across the dunes. The one that looks like it matches this one."

"Yes. The unfriendly guys we talked about last night. And they spoke to you in English?" Ty squinted at me with interest.

"Yes. Loud and clear. I was pretty shaky when I got here. And now, J's gone. I guess it all crashed in on me," I sniffed, blowing my nose loudly.

"Before I forget, there was a phone call from your dad. I saw the message on the pad." Ty looked at me expectantly.

"I took care of that already," I replied flatly.

"Well, let's dress your leg wound. I can practice my Boy Scout skills." Ty led me across the yard to the kitchen.

"Uh, will I ever walk again?" I kidded.

"Never insult the doctor, young lady," Ty admonished as he picked me up and sat me on the counter. Running through some cabinets, he came up with peroxide, first-aid cream, and giant Band-Aids. In a few stinging swipes, he had me disinfected and bandaged.

"Thanks," I said blowing my nose again.

"Is there anything else, then, ma'am?" he kidded with an exaggerated bow. His eyes, however, weren't kidding. He stared directly into my eyes, gently insistent on an answer.

"It's just … I wish … I don't get along with my parents, Ty," I finally blurted out. "That call from my father upset me, too. My mom's in the hospital, and he wants me to call her. He's on his way to England. He's not home much." I felt the resentment rising.

"I hope it's nothing serious with your mom." Ty expressed concern.

"Oh, it's serious all right. But, it's also chronic. I'm used to her being in the hospital a lot."

"Then you must end up visiting her a lot," said Ty.

I swallowed hard and took a deep breath. I'd gone this far. I might as well go all the way. It would be a relief to tell someone. "She's in an alcoholism rehab, Ty. She has a bad drinking problem. She's okay for a while and then there's some crisis, and she's back in the rehab. She's a charter member of the Betty Ford Clinic. I should be used to it, but somehow I have never become used to it." I snickered, feeling my bitterness all the more, now that the tale was told. Folding my arms, I turned away, embarrassed, ashamed.

"What was it that upset you more than usual?" Ty asked.

"I can't bring myself to talk to her. I can't help but think she could stop if she really wanted to." I picked at my bandaged leg, wondering, for the zillionth time, why Dad and I weren't enough reason for Mom to stop drinking.

Ty hoisted himself up on the counter next to me and put his arm around me. "You've had a tough day, Annie. I'm sorry."

His arm felt warm. I put my head on his shoulder and then, without warning, I started to cry in earnest. He put both arms around me, and we rocked together until the tears let up.

"Feel better?" he said, cupping my chin in his hand. I nodded. "Then go wash your face, and we'll have some dinner. The world will improve when you've had some Fire Island chili."

"I love chili. Are we eating now? Where's Doc?" I inquired, getting my tears under control.

"Doc's gone to Bay Shore tonight. We're on our own, and I'm taking you out to dinner. Unless you have another date, that is."

"Yes. I must call the other five men who've been pacing outside my door and blow them off. After all, you are the only admirer of mine who knows a ghost."

Chapter 7
The Ghost Shows Up

"Oh, that chili was hot, Ty. My lips are still burning." We were on a small motor launch known as a water taxi that takes people from one community to another on the island.

After demolishing our bowls of chili in a little café in Ocean Beach, we watched the sunset and decided to head back to Point-O-Woods, where we would meet Alice at 11 o'clock to prepare for our ghost watch.

"How do you prepare for a ghost watch, Ty?" I asked, leaning comfortably against him as we zipped along the shore to the little mooring where Doc's boat was.

"Alice will want you to cleanse your mind so that you're open to the spirit world," Ty replied.

"How do you do that?" I looked up at him, noting how thick and dark his eyelashes were, how his eyebrows came together as he squinted into the distance.

"I don't know, Annie. I pretty much let Alice ramble on, and I see the ghost the same as she does. Maybe this ghost likes uncleansed minds," he offered.

I wondered if Ty would ever say anything to me about his parents. I didn't want to talk to him about my parents at first. But now that he knew about them, I wanted to talk. Here was someone my own age who had the same kind of experiences as I. But, I couldn't very well let on to him what J had revealed to me. I just had to play the waiting game to see what would happen.

The water taxi let us off on the dock at Point-O-Woods. Ty checked on *Star*, tugging a line here and there to make sure all was well. It was 10 PM, which gave us enough time to stop at Windalee on the way to Alice's.

"You better grab a sweatshirt. It gets chilly on the beach at night, and I see the fog rolling in already. I'm going to check the phone messages, and since no one will be home, I want to lock up, especially your end of the house. No sense taking any chances."

"Any reason for all this caution?" I asked.

"I don't know. Can't be too careful," he smiled at me.

Taking care of business took a few minutes and then we took the boardwalk toward Alice's. It was lovely on the walk at night. Small, low lights intermittently illuminated the path. In some places, the trees growing on the side of the walk made a leafy tunnel. As we walked along, the din of the insects quieted at our approach, only to resume with our passage.

"That next one is your ugly neighbor's house, right?" I was glad Ty was next to me.

"Looks dark and buttoned up to me," Ty observed. Only the pathway lights showed around the little house.

Having learned my lesson this afternoon, I was looking at the boardwalk as we made our way along. Something glistened in the light. At first, I thought it was moisture, but then, why just in that spot? I kept watching as we passed; the little gleam became discernible as a metallic object. Curious, I bent down to see it more clearly.

"What are you doing, looking for grounds to sue these guys?" Ty kidded.

"No, there's a piece of jewelry stuck in the crack between the boards here," I said, prying at it with a coin I had taken from my pocket. When the object finally came loose, I held it up to the light. My heart stopped.

"Oh my God, that's one of J's earrings!" I was astonished. Slowly, but relentlessly, a cold fear gripped me. J could have walked here yesterday and lost the earring. Just because it was here in front of the ugly neighbor's house, it didn't mean anything dire, but still, I couldn't shake my feeling of dread.

"Are you sure?" Ty asked, peering over my shoulder. "Could it just be a similar one?"

"No, these were a special gift from her friends on the force. See the little J in diamond chips?"

"She must have lost it here yesterday," Ty shrugged. "You look like you've already seen a ghost," he added. "Do you still want to go ghost watching?"

"Yeah, I'm sure it's okay. She went back to the city," I said, shaking off the chill. "I'm glad I found it."

We continued on the way to Alice's. I made up my mind to call the city tomorrow to check on J. Sometimes I couldn't contact her directly, but at least I could find out if she was safe.

Alice's house sat amid the dunes, a dark, crouching structure. The house appeared unlit, unusually dark for a house that awaited guests. As we got closer, a yellowish glow seemed to take form in the windows.

The golden color was generated by numerous tiny flames. Candles, of course. What better way to prepare for a ghost sighting?

"Alice has pulled out all the stops for you, Annie," Ty smiled. Even if we don't see M. G. tonight, this will be an experience."

Alice met us at the door dressed in gray sweats. I wondered if those were her ghost bustin' duds.

"Before we go out to the dunes, I'd like you to learn as much about M. G. as you can, Annie. It might help you to tune into her spirit, so to speak. I have collected a fair amount of documented historical data as well as some anecdotal personal accounts I've managed to find in the files of the local newspapers."

"Yes, I'd be really interested in that, Alice. Thanks."

"I'll just go in and try to blow out all the candles one by one. Okay, Alice?" Ty teased.

"Igor and Ivan need walking, if you don't mind," Alice shot back.

"Those are the dogs," Ty whispered and left to find the noble beasts.

Alice had a small office in the back of the house, which was well lit and all business. She gestured me toward a chair. I sat down at the desk.

Two manila envelopes, one marked "hist.," the other marked "pers.," were spread out before me.

I picked up the "hist." and started to leaf through the materials carefully. These were the same kinds of things I had seen in the manila envelope on my first visit. As I leafed through them, they added very little to what I knew, until the last and most recently dated article, headlined "Grieving Husband Exhumes Bodies of Wife and Child." The article gave a name to M. G., her husband, and baby.

Jan Van Thaden has exhumed the remains of his beloved wife and child, Anna and baby Miep. He has moved his fishing operation from Sayville to the island, stating that he felt that Anna could rest there more easily.

The article went on to relate the details of the tragedy.

"Alice, does anyone know where the actual graves are?" This seemed to be a key piece of information. "Are ghosts more likely to be sighted in the vicinity of these graves?" I couldn't believe I was asking such a question. I still wasn't sure if I believed in ghosts. The idea of them caught my imagination, but my practical side rejected the idea. My sense of the ridiculous tried to grapple with the idea of all these spirits inhabiting an already overcrowded world. Who knows? Maybe that empty subway seat I was in the habit of taking was already occupied by someone from the spirit world.

"There is a complicating factor in the story, Annie. During the 1920s, when smuggling alcoholic beverages across Fire Island was as active as any legitimate business, there were a lot of tunnels dug to avoid detection. In my research, I've found out that the grave was probably destroyed.

"Jan Von Thaden had, of course, died long before the twenties. He had no heirs, no one bought his business. So his holdings fell to ruin. The grave went uncared for. It was originally marked by a small flat stone. It may still be here on the island. I've searched in the areas where the grave might have been and found nothing. The most distinct possibility is that the grave was destroyed by the tunnel diggers. Its specific original location is not documented anywhere that I can find."

"How sad," I breathed. "But still, the grave was here on the island."

"Read on, Annie. It's getting late," Alice admonished.

The anecdotal records all gave similar reports. A low moaning sound came from above us, causing my small hairs to stand on end. Alice and I stared at each other, the contents of the folders slipping to the floor.

Alice jumped to her feet, a determined look on her face. "Ty," she yelled. "You'll be responsible for my hair falling out. It's already gray!"

Ty swooped into the room wrapped in one of Alice's colorful throws, a towel wrapped turban-style around his head. "I smell a ghost in the area," he declared in a wavering falsetto voice, eyes closed and arms flapping.

"Ghosts don't smell, you foolish clown. You scared us half to death."

"Ty, those are definitely your colors," I said with a mock intimate wink. I couldn't help laughing, and soon Alice joined in.

"Well kids," she said at last, "it's time. I'm going upstairs for a while to do some deep-breathing exercises. You can join me if you like. It helps to be relaxed." With that, Alice went into the candle room.

Ty and I looked at each other and shrugged. "You look pretty cleansed to me," Ty said, brushing at himself, "How do I look? Do I pass?"

"Yes." I smiled broadly, thinking, *You pass and then some.* I overcame the overwhelming urge to reach up and kiss him.

Ty grabbed my hand and, as we headed for the door, yelled behind us, "Meet you in the dunes, Alice. Last one there is a rotten corpse."

Ugh, I thought.

"Yeah, I know. I should save cracks like that for Halloween." Ty shrugged and pulled me out the door. There was no moon; the dunes appeared dark and shadowy. Most of the lights in the neighboring houses were out by this time, enhancing the lonely, forbidden feeling. The surf hissed and boomed in the distance, sounding closer because of the thickening mist. The breakers were barely discernible at this point.

Ty led us to a depression between two dunes. We spread the throw Ty had appropriated for a costume and settled in for the wait. Alice came along shortly, and we tried to be as comfortable as possible.

"It's probably more efficient if we take turns watching the surf to see if our ghost will emerge," Alice suggested, snuggling down into our little hollow.

"I'll take the first watch," declared Alice. "When I get tired, one of you can take over."

Alice took our silence as approval. Settling in as well as I could in this damp place, I looked up. As the wisps of fog drifted by, there was an occasional glimpse of the moonless sky.

"Look at all those stars!" I exclaimed in a loud whisper. Then, clamping my hand over my mouth, I looked sheepishly at my two companions. "Sorry." I became lost in the mystery of the beach, the softening effect of the fog on the landscape, the hypnotic sound of the surf, the elusive stars. But most of all, the anticipation of a ghost materializing at any moment. Next to me, Ty, too, seemed lost in this vaporous world.

In a short while, the surf and the fog worked their spell on me. I found my eyelids drooping, and before I knew it, I found myself startled awake by a cold hard grip on my arm.

"Shhhh," came the warning in my ear.

Instantly awake, I turned my gaze in the direction Ty was pointing with his other hand. I saw a bright, hazy form flitting along the surf line. The form faded in and out of the fog.

"What is it?" I whispered directly into Ty's ear.

His answer was to cover my mouth with a gentle but firm hand. From the pressure of his hands, I knew that the glowing form was our ghost. Alice was also fixed in place, her face a frozen study in concentration.

The figure began to come away from the surf line, heading toward us. Breathing didn't seem to be an option. I was feeling a growing urge to run. Ty tightened his grip, our eyes riveted on the approaching figure.

As the figure neared, the form took on more distinct features. It was a figure molded from a brown cloak or shroud completely covering the body. No face, hands, or feet were visible. At first, I thought the ghost carried a lantern, but the glow came from somewhere within. The ghost appeared to be clutching something close to its body.

It reminded me of those plastic Statue of Liberty night lamps that have a bulb inside. The ghost passed about twenty yards from us and headed inland.

Alice wasted no time following her, being careful to be quiet. Ty pulled me along after her.

My legs wobbled. One had fallen asleep. The other wished it was asleep and that its owner was the same way: home and in bed.

Our quarry was slipping into the fog. We were having a hard time keeping up. The ghost made it to the boardwalk and started down one of the lanes. *We're losing her,* I thought in a panic. Alice seemed particularly disturbed by the ghost's flight. She put on an extra burst of speed and vaulted herself onto the walkway. We weren't far behind.

There she was, about three hundred feet ahead of us. We were gaining on her. I didn't know if I really wanted to catch up to her.

Suddenly, she was gone. We rushed up to the spot where she had disappeared. Ty dove off the walkway into the brush of someone's yard. I did the same on the other side. Alice seemed to be searching the walkway for some trace of M. G.'s ectoplasm. That's what ghosts were supposed to be made of. I read that somewhere. After about five minutes, we gave up, and the first audible words were spoken.

"This is the same place, isn't it, Ty?" gasped Alice, winded from her effort.

"Yeah, she did it again. At least she's consistent," answered Ty.

"Maybe we got too close?" I remarked lamely. I was shaking all over. "How come you're so calm?" I complained. "That was a ghost, wasn't it?" I felt stupid.

"Don't ghosts run on some sort of energy? Maybe hers ran out," I added another helpful remark.

"Well, they're not exactly Eveready batteries, Annie. But that could be a possible explanation. It still doesn't explain why she heads in this direction every time," Ty explained.

"Annie, I'd like to go back to my house and check the list Ty and I have been keeping on these sightings," Alice said.

"Let's get out of this dampness," said Ty. "We need to calm down and decompress from this."

At Alice's, we all had a hot drink to warm ourselves. Finally, I stopped shaking. Alice began to go through her checklist.

"Ty, did you notice anything at all that was new or different this time?" she inquired.

Ty put his face in his hands and thought for a while. "No, I can't think of anything." Ty replied, shaking his head.

"Annie, what did you see? Try to include every detail. Either things you saw or things you would have expected to see knowing M. G.'s history." Alice was scanning her list.

I recounted what I saw. She grunted assent as she checked her list. "But I never saw the baby," I concluded. "She appeared to be clutching something, but I couldn't tell if it was a baby. It did stick in my mind. I thought the baby would be more obvious."

"Hmm, I never thought of that," Ty mused.

Alice closed her notebook with a snap. "Let's call it a night, kids. It's 2:30."

Ty placed my sweatshirt around my shoulders as he stifled a yawn. We bid Alice good night and headed home to Windalee.

When we reached the cottage, we saw lights everywhere. Doc was home.

"Listen, you can have the spare room on our side if you're afraid to sleep here alone tonight, Annie."

"No. It's okay. I'm too tired to be scared."

I looked up at Ty to say good night. He turned to me, and we were very close, nose to nose as they say.

I could feel his breath ruffling the stray hairs around my face. His eyes found mine, as he slid his arms around me. His eyes closed. Our mouths found each other, and we were lost in that inevitable kiss. The one I'd felt coming all day. It was a long kiss, melting away the tension that came from its not happening sooner.

At last Ty pulled away, looking into my eyes. *Don't let go of me now*, I thought. With that, I pulled his head down to kiss him again.

"Good night, Annie," he said. His voice cracked a little. "Come over for breakfast in the morning. We'll go sailing."

I stood there, watching him go, feeling that he had taken the inside of me with him and leaving this tired shell of a body here on the steps of Windalee.

Chapter 8
A Thief in Paradise

I WANDERED THROUGH THE HOUSE, turning off the lights. In the bathroom, I looked at my face in the mirror. Did it change any since I landed on this island with its mystery and danger and, well yes, Ty? Same light brown hair, maybe a little sun streaked now, same green eyes. The nose and lips are in the same place, but sunburned. Did I look a little older, possibly more sophisticated? I brushed my teeth, undressed, and went to bed.

Staring at the ceiling, I tried not to let in any thoughts. I just kept reliving that kiss. My body felt light and insubstantial. My mouth could still feel Ty's lips; my ears could hear his breath. I thought about his hands, tan and strong, but how gentle he was with me. *I can't leave here,* I thought. I don't want to ever go away from this place, and Ty, and the magic I was feeling. I drifted off to sleep, cherishing that first kiss.

The dream evaporated with the morning sun, streaming into the room. Something important was supposed to happen today. I tried to clear my foggy brain to remember what it was. *Ty,* I thought. Images began to emerge: the Madonna Ghost, J's earring, Ty, the kiss. I rubbed my eyes. Remembering last night, I hugged the pillow and tried to return to that place. Merlin barked and I remembered. I wanted to check to see if J was okay. And Ty wanted to go sailing.

I pushed myself out of bed and showered. As the hot water soothed my body, I thought of how to contact J. I'd have to call her office. If she wasn't there, I'd have to get hold of Lt. Red. An icy finger of fear squeezed at my gut.

I made the call. A secretary answered. "Hi Annie, your aunt's outta the office now, dear."

"Is Lt. Red there, Millie?" I asked.

"No, him neither, hon. But I'll leave a message. He said he'd check his messages around noon."

"I won't be here then. Listen, I'll try to call him around then. Bye." The line went dead, and I worried again.

A knock came at the front door, accompanied by the smell of coffee.

"Ready for a sail?" inquired a smiling Ty, laden with muffins and coffee-filled mugs.

"Come on over to the kitchen. I'm just packing us some lunch. I could use some help." Cramming my wallet with Lt. Red's number into my shorts, and grabbing a sweatshirt, I took a mug from Ty and shut the door. The muffins were as good as they smelled. I ate one quickly while we packed lunch.

We cleaned up, put out the cats, and headed for the dock, with Merlin yapping at our heels.

"Merlin, you deserve a sail. Good boy," Ty said as he playfully ruffled the dog's ears.

"Isn't he afraid of the boat?" I asked.

"He loves the boat, Annie." With that, Merlin barked and sat up. Ty tossed him a dog treat, and we were on our way.

"I hope you're ready for another sailing lesson, because you're going to sail the boat home yourself," admonished Ty.

"Yes, but will I be able to get cell phone service on the boat around noon?" I asked. I wanted to spend the day sailing, but I was concerned. I hoped I didn't sound like I didn't want to go.

"You look worried, Annie. Still wondering about your aunt?"

"A bit," I admitted.

"Well, we can make it across the bay by noon, and there's a phone on the gas dock if your cell won't work, okay?"

"Oh, great!" I smiled my relief. We walked along in silence, laughing at Merlin's doggy antics.

The path became more crowded as we approached the marina, with its smattering of shops.

"What the …?" Ty muttered, standing on tiptoe, looking toward the slip where *Star* was docked.

On the pier, we could see the flashing light of the marine police boat and a small crowd gathering. Ty snapped a leash on Merlin, and we rushed over to see what the fuss was about.

The center of activity was *Star*. Doc was standing in the cockpit, talking earnestly with a police officer. Another police officer was taping off access to the boat. We ran up to the yellow tape, Ty breathlessly explaining that Doc was his uncle.

"Wait here," the officer commanded and went off to speak to Doc and the other officer. After a few words, he signaled us to come ahead.

"What happened?" demanded Ty. "Are you okay?" I added, scrutinizing Doc carefully.

"It seems that someone borrowed *Star* last night," explained Doc. "When I came aboard this morning, she was only tied with one line. Thank God, she didn't get loose and that the wind kept her up against the pilings."

"Any damage?" asked Ty.

"Just the paint job up on the bow. Take a look," Doc gestured, looking fierce.

"Don't touch anything, son," admonished the police officer.

"We came by here last night around ten, and everything was okay then," I offered.

"Yes, and I was by at 12:00, when I got off the ferry. The radio's missing, too," Doc looked at the police officer.

"Right now, I'd like you all to leave the boat without touching anything." The police officer ushered us off the boat.

"When will we be free to use the boat?" asked Doc, eyeing our picnic basket.

"You can pretty much forget today. Crime scene has to finish up a robbery in Brentwood before they come here." The police officer dispensed with our day of sailing with that simple statement.

Ty and I tried to hide our disappointment by offering, "Doc, do you need any help?"

"Can't do a thing until the boat's not a crime scene anymore," he replied.

The three of us stared at the boat, formulating our separate theories of what had happened. The number of odd things that had happened here in three days was beginning to prickle my instincts. Did they have anything to do with each other?

"Well, I'm going back to the house," Doc announced. "Bye, kids."

Ty seemed to be lost in his own world. All of a sudden, he roused himself and started after Doc in a hurry.

"Doc, can you take this back to the house?" he asked, anxiously handing over the basket. "I have someplace I want to take Annie."

Doc looked up at Ty intently for a moment and then replied, "Sure, Ty, see you for dinner?"

"Yeah, thanks Doc." Doc clapped Ty on the arm.

"Annie, I want you to meet someone. I've been thinking a lot about it, and it could be interesting for you. We have to take the ferry into Bay Shore."

"Well, who is it? Where are we going?" I asked, feeling curious and worried at the same time.

Ty looked me straight in the eye. "I want you to meet my dad, Annie. He's in the psychiatric ward at Central Islip Hospital. He's physically and mentally disabled from his drinking. I visit him about once a week. He likes to meet my friends."

"I don't know, Ty. This is embarrassing." I suddenly felt confused and frightened. So, the mental hospital was for alcoholism. Here I was, wondering if Ty would ever talk about his parents, and now he wanted me to come see his dad. I did not want to go to a hospital to visit an alcoholic. Too close to home. I might end up having to see my mother. All the old flight mechanisms were pulling at me to run for my life from this situation.

Ty looked hard at me again. "Annie, I'm not going to force you. But, you shared your feelings about your parents with me. I'd like to share how I cope with mine with you. I'm no saint, Annie. It took a while for me to visit Dad. I felt just like you, maybe worse. Now, I'm glad I do it. It makes me feel better about the situation—believe it or not."

I didn't expect this. I wished I had more time to think about it. The confrontation with Dad over Mom was looming. I had just kept putting it aside.

"Do you stay long?" I asked, feeling myself caving in.

"No, he has a real short attention span. So, the visits are short. But, he always seems glad to see me."

If I change my mind, can I wait outside?" I negotiated.

"Nobody's going to make you do anything you don't want to, Annie," Ty assured me.

"Okay, then. I'll go," I decided, taking a deep breath and thinking with dread, *I'm not going to like this at all. I'm just doing this to please Ty,* I reasoned.

We hopped onto the ferry, which got us into Bay Shore, where we took a bus that took us across Long Island to Central Islip.

"My dad drank so much that he used to pass out," Ty began as the bus chugged along. Staring straight ahead, he continued, "He smoked, too. That's how my mother died. One of his cigarettes set the couch on fire. The firefighters got him out, but my mom was already dead from smoke inhalation. I wasn't home," he finished, his voice flat.

"Don't you hate him?" I asked. "How can you stand the sight of him?"

"I couldn't for a long, long time," Ty said. "Seeing him here helps me to understand that he's a very sick man."

"Ugh," I said hugging myself from the emotional chill of his story.

We fell silent, retreating into our personal thoughts. The silence made me more nervous, and, at last, I broke the silence and tried to change the mood.

"Was that really a ghost we saw last night? It wasn't what I expected at all."

"I had my doubts at first, too. I thought we were missing some important factor that would give some absolutely plausible explanation," Ty explained.

"It sounds like you've come over to the ghost's side?" I asked.

"We have eliminated every other possibility so far, Annie. I'm not convinced it's a ghost. I just don't have another explanation," Ty shrugged.

"I always loved ghost stories for that reason. No one seems to be able to give a reasonable explanation. I love the mystery of it all. But now that I have my own real-life ghost phenomenon, I want to give it a reasonable explanation. I want her to be a sleepwalker, a local playing a hoax on Alice, anything."

"That's just your logical side taking over. You're just a product of your education," offered Ty.

"Alice is convinced that what we saw last night is the real thing. As you can see, she's keeping a file on the Madonna Ghost, background research. She makes anecdotal records of every sighting. She wants to present all this documentation to the same paranormal experts who came here last time," Ty added.

"Didn't they scare Madonna Ghost away, though?" I asked.

"So the locals like to joke. Alice feels that if she gives them enough information, they'll be able to figure out a way to record a sighting without frightening her off."

"That part interests me," I stated.

"Quite the scientist, eh Annie," Ty quipped, pulling my hat over my eyes. I punched him playfully, as he searched for the buzzer to signal the driver for our stop.

My stomach did a flip-flop as we alit from the bus. The hospital was an ugly institutional building made of red brick. Heavy wire mesh covered the outside of all the windows. I gritted my teeth, expecting to hear screams and moans from the windows.

We entered the lobby. People were sitting in the waiting room area, buying food at a snack bar and generally milling around.

"A lot of people you see are patients, Annie," claimed Ty. "They have one of those shoplifting buttons on, and if they go through the door, it alerts the security guard. Otherwise, they can wander about this commons area. Do you want to wait for me here?"

I looked around nervously. "Uh, no, I'll go with you," I replied, not wanting to stay alone. We took the elevator to Ty's father's floor, and the nurse waved us through to the sitting room, where Ty showed her his pass.

The sitting room was puke green with a gray linoleum floor. Functional chairs stood in groups or lined the walls. A TV chattered away from its perch high on the wall.

Ty made his way across the room, taking me by the hand. His

quarry was a very thin man sitting in a leatherette easy chair. As we approached, I could see Ty's resemblance to him. He must have been very handsome once. Now he was gray. Not just his hair, his whole demeanor. He stared vacantly at the TV, all the while chewing on a wooden coffee stirrer.

"Hi, Dad. I'd like you to meet a friend of mine," Ty called out cheerfully.

Hearing his son's voice, I saw Mr. Egan's face transform itself. The vacant, bored eyes lit with a warmth that gave away his feelings for Ty.

"Ty, my boy," came a lyrical voice. "A sight for sore eyes," he added in a hint of Irish brogue.

"Save your blarney for Miss Annie Tillery, Dad," Ty smiled.

"My pleasure, lass." He gripped my hand with his dry one. His eyes searched my face, and I caught his sadness.

"Pleased to meet you, Mr. Egan," I said in my most polite tone. It was difficult not to be charmed by this man, even though he was more a shadow than a vital man.

"And where are you from, Miss Annie Tillery?" he inquired, letting go of my hand and gesturing Ty and myself into chairs.

"My aunt and I are vacationing on Fire Island. We're staying with Doc and Ty at Windalee. My aunt knows Doc from her work," I offered.

"Do you go to school together, then?" he asked, seeming to ignore my reply.

"No, Dad. She's a visitor on the island," said Ty in a simple firm way.

"Oh, yes, yes. I see," Mr. Egan replied enthusiastically, but looked away in confusion. He started rubbing his hands together nervously. I looked at his hands, noticing the shiny skin and discoloration. I wondered if these were burn scars.

"Did you watch the Mets game, Dad?" Ty asked, trying to help his father through some rough spot that he seemed to understand.

"Oh, yes, I did. The dopes lost again," he added dejectedly. "But the Yankees are on a winning streak." He seemed to cheer up at the idea of it.

"Do you follow baseball, then, Annie?" he turned to me.

"Oh, I love the Mets," I smiled, lying. "But my real love is hockey. I'm a Rangers fan," I announced with pride.

"Savages, to a man," spat out Mr. Egan with spirit. After a minute, he added, "But to each his own."

"Dad, do you need anything?"

"Can you get me a pack of Camels, Ty?" he said conspiratorially.

"You know you can't smoke in here, Dad. Remember, it's against the rules."

Mr. Egan frowned, rubbing his hands together again. He seemed to be trying to remember something, something that made him frightened or worried. With that, he turned again to the TV, the light in his eyes blinking out. I thought of that expression, "nice house—nobody home."

"Well, Dad, it's been great seeing you. I'll be back soon." Ty brought the visit to a conclusion, none too soon for me. He stopped at the nurses' station to ask about his father's physical condition.

As I waited, I kept thinking about my mother, how she had that same look about her, as if she just couldn't manage to jump into the fray that people call life. She always seemed to be seeking some refuge, some escape. I used to think that I was the thing she wanted to get away from. But, after seeing Mr. Egan, I began to wonder if what scared them was just anything that made you feel. I tried to imagine not wanting to feel about the things that happened in life. I couldn't. I just couldn't imagine the place that Mr. Egan and Mom inhabited. It frightened and disgusted me in turn every time I did think about it.

Finally, Ty came away from the nurses' station, looking me over, trying to appraise my mood. He looked older to me, shoulders hunched, hands jammed into pockets. What an awful responsibility he had taken on. I only wanted to run away from a similar one.

"Could we go home now?" I asked. It sounded like a big baby even to me. I tried to overcome my embarrassment.

"Okay. I guess this wasn't such a great idea," Ty consented, nodding toward the door.

"You're wrong, Ty. You are a saint. I couldn't do this. I'm too angry," I said, trying to smooth over things. "This confuses me terribly. How can you be so good to him after all the grief he's caused? Help me out here. I don't understand."

"Pretend you're watching a TV show and you don't know your mother. Look at her as if she is character in a drama. Do you envy her life? Would you want to be her?"

I ran the scene Ty described in my brain's DVD player. I could sort of see what he meant. "But she has caused so much unhappiness!" I shot back.

"How does she change your day-to-day life, Annie?" he asked quietly. "I see my dad as pitiful. Anyone who has no control over their lives is pitiful. I walk in and out of this hospital as I please. I'm not sure he even knows where the door is."

The bus came. We retreated into silence. Ty said, "Think about it, Annie. I had to think about it for a long time. I still do have to think about it."

Suddenly, he put his arm around me. "And I owe you a sail. Will you settle for a frozen yogurt in Bay Shore?" He smiled that dazzling grin.

I laughed, tucking my arm behind him and hooking my finger in one of his belt loops.

Chapter 9
Going Underground

THE FERRY BUMPED INTO POINT-O-WOODS marina, jiggling a loose nut in my brain. "Oh my God!" I gasped, jumping out of my seat, scanning the dock furiously.

"What?" Ty rushed to my side.

"I forgot to call Lt. Red. What time is it? My cell won't work here. Good, there are phones on the dock, I'll call right away. Maybe I will catch someone in."

"It's 4:30. Do you have time?" Ty rummaged in his pockets for change.

Once on the dock with the change we managed to scrape up between us, I placed the call. Ty looked on anxiously.

I heard Millie answer and asked if Lt. Red had left a message, or better, had anyone heard from J.

"Gee, honey, Red never came back to the office. Your aunt's on special assignment, so she doesn't check in here. She has a contact person."

"Thanks," I replied dejectedly, that now-dreaded word "contact" leaping out at me again.

I returned the receiver and leaned against the phone booth, closing my eyes. I tried to remember if I had Lt. Red's home phone number.

"No luck?" Ty read my face.

"It's unlike her not to leave me a message every other day or so."

"Maybe she left a message at Windalee," Ty offered.

"Maybe so." My spirits rose a bit as we walked home.

Once at Windalee, he headed straight for the answering machine. Doc was in the kitchen with a visitor. They were bent over some papers on the kitchen table; their steaming cups of coffee filled the room with a mocha aroma.

Two heads came up as the screen door slammed, and to my surprise, it was Alice who sat at the table with Doc.

"There's a message for you on the answering machine, Annie. I wound it back for you, so you could hear it firsthand," Doc gave the good news.

"Thanks!" My hopes soared.

I pressed the "message" button and waited.

"This message is for Annie," came Lt. Red's booming voice. "I haven't heard from Aunt Jill yet, but a message is due in soon. Don't worry." He gave me his home phone number and signed off.

Suddenly, I felt tired. This wasn't the message I wanted to hear. But, Lt. Red was right. I should hear soon. I tried to shake off the uneasy feeling, becoming aware that the other inhabitants of the kitchen were engrossed in the documents spread out on the kitchen table.

"What is that? Some pirate's treasure map? Will it make us rich?" I teased as I elbowed my way between Ty and Doc.

"These papers are land surveys prepared for the Suffolk County Police Department in 1928," Alice explained. "I have a cousin who is a retired Suffolk County police officer. His beat was Fire Island during the Prohibition days. He knows how interested I am in Fire Island history. So, he gave me a whole box of junk he had from his police days."

"And, bingo! We have these," Alice made a sweeping gesture of triumph, causing Merlin to run to the door, growling.

"What's wrong with him?" muttered Ty. "He's jumpy tonight."

"Must be all this ghost talk, folks," Doc declared. "You're making a neurotic out of him."

Merlin ran back and jumped on Doc's lap, eliciting a grunt.

"I think these maps are important, because they may help us locate

Madonna Ghost's grave. I've spent the afternoon in Town Hall, getting the actual locations of the lots marked on the survey."

"Oh, I see," I exclaimed as I read her light pencil notes. "This is your house, and, hmm … here's Windalee."

"The dotted lines are the tunnels," explained Doc as he ran a ruler along the survey, trying to make sense of the maze of tunnels. "This one here is the one I boarded up," Doc pointed.

Alice squinted at the survey, measuring distances with her thumb. "I'm trying to figure out where the exact spot is that our ghost drops out of sight. I would have to go measure the actual boardwalk distance and use this scale that's on the survey," she pointed out.

"The boardwalk was built in 1958. You can't use it for a reference point in these diagrams," Doc added.

"We'll have to figure out where to put it in the survey by measuring from the houses that were there then and now," Ty mused.

"That shouldn't be hard. It's a good couple of hours' work." Doc looked at Ty and me.

"Doc, can you let us see your tunnel? Is the one you boarded up safe to explore?" asked Alice.

"Yes, it's quite sound. I boarded it up, because I didn't want any winter vandals getting into the place and the cottage through there. I did a real good job of camouflaging the entrance." Doc went over to the closet and took out a pry bar, gesturing for us to follow. Ty grabbed a hammer, and we all filed out into the gathering gloom.

"One of you get some flashlights," Doc called back.

"I'll get them if you tell me where they are," I offered.

"In that same closet that Doc went into, Annie," Ty answered. I ran back and opened the closet. I found the flashlights easily enough, but as I went to close the door, I noticed a row of labeled keys on hooks. One in particular tweaked at my curiosity, the one with a tag that said "cottage."

Shrugging off the momentary distraction, I rushed to join our little expedition. Doc had already removed the brush-like plants he'd placed in front of the boarded-up tunnel. Behind the plants was a cleverly draped section of snow fence, which Ty, Alice, and Doc were untangling.

At last, the boards were accessible and ready to be pried loose. The nails gave way with their usual screech of protest, and the tunnel was open to us.

I handed everyone a flashlight, and Doc cautiously led the way.

The tunnel was shored up in places with pieces of lumber. In some spots, the sand was land sliding into the tunnel.

"It was only possible to dig these tunnels where there was a deposit of subsoil under the sand. The subsoil is very hard. Otherwise, they would have caved in long ago is my guess." Doc continued down the tunnel, his voice made strange by the closeness of the walls.

Flashlight beams made a light show, bouncing everywhere. Small scuttling noises could be heard from the dark shadows.

"Oh, those aren't rats, are they?" I shuddered involuntarily at the thought of it.

"No, Annie. They're land crabs. Harmless. Don't worry," came Ty's soothing voice. I grabbed his hand.

"How far does this tunnel go, Doc? I'm getting a little claustrophobic." Alice's voice quivered a little, echoing the feelings of all of us.

"Only about two hundred feet more, Alice. I can see my barricade up ahead."

Doc had used the existing timbers along the tunnel wall and ceiling as a framework to nail plywood sections, making a strong barrier.

"How much further does the tunnel go beyond the barricade?" asked Alice.

"It comes out very close to the cottage. I don't remember exactly where, but I would say another fifty feet," came Doc's reply.

"Damn! I wish I had remembered to bring a compass and measuring tape!" exclaimed Alice. "I want to know exactly where this tunnel comes up."

"We can take those measurements for you tomorrow," Ty offered. "It would be better to do that in the daytime anyway."

"Can we get through this barrier then, Doc?" Alice persisted.

"Must we, Alice?" Doc asked a little impatiently.

"Yes, if whoever we see disappearing on the boardwalk near the cottage is coming down into the tunnel, there might be some signs of them. Especially if it's not a ghost. Don't you want to know who might be coming down into this tunnel? It's on your property." Alice held firm, staring at Doc.

"Do you think it might not be a ghost?" asked Doc with mock surprise.

"Well, I'd really like to know for sure, ghost or no ghost," Alice countered.

"Ty, help me with this lumber," Doc sighed.

Alice and I stepped back, holding the flashlights high so that Ty and Doc could see.

Alice's shaking hand caused the light to waver, increasing the eeriness of the scene. To Doc's surprise, his barricade came away with little effort, while dust mites danced in the flashlight beams. "Someone who doesn't belong has been in here."

Carefully, we picked our way over the rubble and onto the other side of the barrier.

"Everyone, take a section of the tunnel and search it carefully," ordered Alice.

I decided to take the far end just to get out of everyone's way. There was an air of tension created by being in the tunnel that made me uncomfortable.

The far end of the tunnel ended at a blank wall. This made me curious, since Doc had already indicated that you could access the tunnel from this end. I shone my flashlight on the walls and ceiling, walking backward away from the dead end. My light caught what seemed to be a trap door of some kind. My heel hit a large solid object, and I began to fall backward. In the midst of the fall, the flashlight went up in the air, as I lost my grip on it. The next thing I knew, everyone was looking down at me with concern.

"She's okay. Just got the wind knocked out of her," proclaimed Doc. "Can you get up, Annie?"

"Yeah. Sure. I tripped over something big on the floor over there," I grunted, getting up with a hand from Ty.

"Let's see what it is." Ty began to scuffle through the sand on the floor where I fell.

"Here. It's a square piece of stone," Ty said excitedly. "With some writing on it."

Everyone rushed to see what it was. Ty and Doc lifted it out of the sand that it was buried in, laying it writing side up on the floor in the middle of the tunnel.

The letters and numbers were quite faint. But there was enough there to encourage Alice in her conclusion that we had stumbled on the lost grave marker of the Madonna Ghost and her child.

"I must have passed over this a dozen times, and it's half-buried, so I thought it was a rock."

"Can we take this out with us?" Alice almost pleaded.

"I don't see why not," answered Doc. "I do suggest we sift this area as carefully as possible tonight to see if we've missed anything."

We scuffled about as carefully as possible for another half hour. Doc finally called it quits. I made one more sweep with my flashlight, and something glittered in the light.

"Wait, I see something!" I called to the retreating figures.

In the light of all four flashlights, a little gold flash shot sparks of light at us. I went toward it. It was the tiniest speck. Like finding a single pebble in the Grand Canyon.

I picked it up carefully, blowing off the grit. I peered at it, lying in the palm of my hand. It was a gold back for a pierced earring wire.

"What is it, for goodness sakes?" demanded Alice. I showed her.

"Well, that doesn't belong to our ghost. Too modern," she observed.

"Probably comes from somebody who was in here exploring before I boarded it up," said Doc.

"It looks as if it were dropped just yesterday," I mused. "I wonder if the earring is around?" We sifted the sand for a while longer but decided to continue the search tomorrow. I slipped the tiny object into my sweatshirt pocket.

For once, it was silent in the tunnel, as we all paused before leaving. Just as Ty and Doc bent to lift the stone, a strange sound barely vibrated through the tunnel.

"What the heck …," Ty began.

"Shhh," commanded Alice.

The low vibration continued as we listened, rising in cadence and falling off.

Moaning. It sounded like a sad, mournful moan. We looked from one to the other. I thought my ears had grown to four times their normal size so hard was I listening. I gripped Ty's hand so tightly that I must be hurting him. He didn't utter a sound. Alice was moving slowly along the tunnel, trying to locate the source of the sound. When she reached the trap door, she carefully placed her fingertips against it. The sound stopped just as suddenly as it started. We waited. One minute. Another minute. Doc tried to stifle a sneeze. Without a word, stone in hand, we filed out of the tunnel.

Chapter 10
THE PLOT AT GLASS HOUSE

THE SUN HAD LONG SET, and the cool fresh air brought back a sense of reality. By the time we got back to the bright lights of Doc's kitchen, I had my knocking knees under control. Alice had composed herself enough to say in an almost normal voice, "We need to do some authentication before we decide what our tunnel experience was all about. I can't help but feel the Madonna Ghost comes back to visit the grave of her child. I believe that could have been her spirit moaning," she declared.

"It could have been the breeze in the tunnel," countered Doc. "But, you're right. Let's find out if the stone is what we think it is."

"Where exactly does that trap door in the tunnel lead to?" Alice inquired of Doc.

"I'm not sure if it's in the cottage or just on the cottage property," Doc replied. "I couldn't get it open from the tunnel side, and I never did see any trap door in the cottage."

"We'll find out where it leads tomorrow by measuring the length of the tunnel and taking a compass heading," said Ty, rummaging in a drawer to find the necessary gear for the task.

"How can you prove the stone is our grave marker?" I asked, stifling a yawn.

"I'm going to call my friend Harry McKnight from the Long Island

Historical Society. He'll know." Alice seemed very satisfied with the night's work and began to fold the survey.

"Let's call it a night, folks," proposed Doc. "Alice, leave the survey. Ty and Annie will bring it back to you in the morning, after they finish their measuring. I don't know about you, but I'm beat."

We grunted our agreement.

"Annie, let me walk you to your room and then I'll walk Alice home," Ty put his arm around me. I leaned on him gratefully, not realizing how tired I was.

Once across the yard, he held me by the shoulders and looked into my eyes.

"You've had quite a day, haven't you? But not really summer vacation stuff, huh?"

"It's the adventure of a lifetime," I protested. "Our very own ghost!"

"Look, as soon as we finish the survey for Alice, let's take *Star* over to Sailor's Haven. It's part of the national forest system. It's neat."

"Whatever you say, captain." I yawned in spite of myself. "I wish J would call. I'm really worried, Ty." I looked up at him, hoping to find an answer in his face. What I saw was another kind of answer.

He kissed me good night and held me for a moment.

"I really care about you, Annie. Get some sleep. Maybe tomorrow will bring some answers."

"Night, Ty," I murmured, barely able to keep awake. I had to get some sleep.

The next morning I slept late. Not on purpose, but the effect was the same. I jumped out of bed when I saw that it was already 11 AM.

Oh, no, I thought. *I've missed everything, I bet!* I threw on some clothes and combed my hair as I ran across the yard to the kitchen.

The big room was empty, my voice producing an echo as I called out to Ty and Doc. A note on the refrigerator caught my attention.

Annie. There's a message on the answering machine for you. I finished the measurements on the survey this morning. Could you deliver it to Alice? Doc and I had to go into Bay Shore to straighten out some police business regarding the boat.
See you later.
Love, Ty

The survey was in a big manila envelope on the counter.

I collapsed into a kitchen chair, deflated. Hurry up and wait. I had missed Ty this morning and felt the disappointment keenly. When would Ty be home?

"The answering machine," I yelled out loud. The message that Ty recorded was from Lt. Red. He said that he expected a message from J any minute. He would be arriving for a visit tomorrow morning.

I replayed the message. *Why is he coming to visit?* I wondered. The same uneasy feeling I'd had since J left Fire Island gripped me. A little sparkle of hope glinted in my mind's eye. *Maybe Lt. Red was bringing J with him. If anything had happened, I would've heard,* I reasoned.

Absently, I poured a glass of milk, trying to make sense of the mysteries of the last few days. I missed J. After four chocolate chip cookies (J would kill me), I decided to make my way over to Alice's Glass House. Closing up at Doc's, I made my way toward the boardwalk, stiffening as I realized that I would be passing the neighbors' house again.

If Alice had gotten an opinion on the stone we found in the tunnel, we could make some attempt at piecing the puzzle together.

Plodding along the walk, I continued to juggle the events of the last few days around in my brain. A loud bang and then a thud caused me to look up. I was abreast of the cottage next door. I stopped. From inside came a muffled voice. I couldn't make out what was being said, but the tone was unmistakable. There was a heated argument in progress. *What is it about this place?* I wondered. *Every time I come by here, something disturbing is going on.* I heard a groan, as something hit the wall nearest me, making the window rattle.

This sounds serious. What should I do? I struggled with myself. *Run away? Eavesdrop? Call the police?*

Suddenly, the door flew open, and one of the neighbors bolted out the door, catching me completely by surprise. For an instant, we stared at each other. My brain was telling my feet to run, but before they got the message, the man reentered the house as quickly as he had exited. The front door slammed; windows banged shut. More muffled yelling punctuated each slam and bang. It was a few seconds before I realized that it had become completely silent. So still, that I could hear the sound of surf from the beach.

Shaking myself into action, I continued my walk, unable to shake off the growing apprehension I felt. The memory of finding J's earring at the very spot I had just left crept into my consciousness, deepening the pit in my stomach.

Getting control of this feeling of dread occupied me until Glass House came into view. Alice let me in, and I presented her with Ty's survey. Her eyes lit up with the excitement of coming closer to solving the ghost mystery, but the light dimmed as she looked into my eyes.

"What on earth is wrong, Annie? I'd say you look like you've seen a ghost, but even when you did, you looked better than you do now."

I related the incident that had just occurred at the neighbors' cottage.

"I'm worried about my aunt, too," I confessed. "I always worry, but I guess finding her earring in front of the cottage has just spooked me. I wish I could think of something to do."

"I know what you mean." Alice's voice was reassuring. "I must admit I've been keeping careful watch on the place myself."

I looked at Alice. She leveled her gaze at me and continued.

"I went by there last night after Ty dropped me off here. There was a lot of shouting going on inside. I could only catch a word here and there, not enough to make any sense out of it. I was about to leave, when I heard a door slam on the other side of the house leading to the backyard."

"Did you see anything?" I interrupted impatiently.

"I tried, Annie. Really, I did. But I didn't want to be seen. I tried to get around on the side, and I did manage to see two men dragging a huge bundle from the back steps into the yard."

"Where did they drag it?" Again, my impatience won.

"I didn't see, Annie. At that moment, another man came out the front door, and I had to drop behind the bushes."

Alice and I looked at each other and fell silent, vague images of evil-doing forming in my mind.

Finally, I offered, "Could we call the police? Aren't they disturbing the peace or something? They sure are disturbing mine."

"Yes, I know what you mean," replied Alice. "I've been looking into town ordinances and the like to see if they have committed any violations that would give us an excuse to call in some authority. I haven't found anything yet."

"Maybe Doc might know. Besides, he rents that cottage, doesn't he?" My hopes rose, thinking this might be our angle.

"The rental is handled through a realtor. So, Doc doesn't have to have anything to do with them," Alice replied.

"But if he suspects they are doing something to damage the house, can't he report it, to get in and see the house?" I demanded, not wanting to let this go.

"I don't know, Annie. Doc is unflappable when it comes to people's privacy. He would have to have a strong reason to intrude on that right to privacy. It's also bad business to be nosy regarding your tenants here on the island. People come here for privacy."

"I'm going to ask him tonight," I declared. "I don't know what I'll do if he says that we ought to mind our own business," I added.

"Well," Alice replied, "I'm going to go by again tonight after my ghost watch. The moon is waxing to full fast, and I figure this to be the last night our Madonna will show herself this month."

"If she does show, you'll end up at the cottage anyway, since that's her vanishing point," I observed.

"Annie!" cried Alice, slapping her forehead. "The survey! Let's see if the tunnel comes up in the neighbors' cottage."

We opened the manila envelope that had been forgotten on the table in front of us. Ty's careful measurements, plotted out on the land survey, showed that the tunnel we had explored last night ended near the backyard of the cottage. It was not possible to tell, however, if the tunnel ended in the backyard or under the boardwalk, since the old land survey didn't show the boardwalk. Ty hadn't entered the location of the walk.

"So, we're back to the neighbors' cottage again," I mused. "We have to go over there now anyway to measure the distance from the house to see where the trap door to the tunnel might be."

"I can't imagine the neighbors will want us anywhere near the place," I continued. "Every time I'm near the place and they see me, they blow a fit."

Alice got up from her chair, rearranging her outfit thoughtfully. "I'll do those measurements tonight. They won't see me doing it, so they can't get annoyed," she decided, her decision made.

"Don't you think that's dangerous?" I asked.

"I don't care. What can they do to me, tell me to buzz off?" Alice looked at me defiantly.

"Look, Alice, these guys could be dangerous," I said emphatically, feeling my own fear. I told her about my first evening on the island and how I had observed the cottage people from the porch at Windalee. I told her about the gun one of them wore.

"Who knows what they're up to," I said, trying to be convincing.

"Let me see if I can get Doc to get them away from the cottage for some reason. While they're away, we can measure," I persuaded.

"And I'll look around inside," Alice stated with resolve. "We'll straighten this out once and for all."

I got up, joining Alice at the window facing the ocean. I remembered J.

"Alice, I'm going back to Windalee. I want to see if my aunt left a message on the phone machine, and I hope Ty and Doc are back."

"Yes. Ask Doc what he thinks about the neighbors. Call me and let me know."

We said good-bye. I returned on the boardwalk path, noting how silent the cottage was as I passed. When I got back to Windalee, Ty and Doc were in the kitchen. Ty looked annoyed.

"Hi," I said, looking curiously at Ty. He returned my greeting unenthusiastically. I felt a pang of rejection.

"We can't go out on the boat this afternoon, Annie. The police still have it as a crime scene."

I had forgotten about the sail we had planned.

"Oh well. Maybe we can just walk the beach over to that other town, Ocean Beach? J said she liked it." I automatically looked at the phone when I said my aunt's name. "Did my aunt call?" I dared to ask, flashing the tension of that question to Ty and Doc.

"No, Annie," replied Doc. "But Lt. Red did. He'll be here on the first ferry in the morning. He promised that he'll have word for you then."

I felt keenly disappointed. I had to wait another day. This was beginning to feel like an un-vacation. I felt tears well up.

"Uh, why do the police still have the boat?" I asked, trying to change the subject and get control of myself.

"They said they might have an ID on one set of prints, and they want to see if there are more of these prints on the boat. They're going to seal off the cabin, which they didn't previously check for prints, and fume it with Super Glue to see if they can get another set of prints."

Ty related this piece of information to me as I watched Doc, trying to see if this would be a good time to ask about investigating our neighbors. He was unreadable. This is as good a time as any, I reasoned, and plunged ahead.

"Doc, what is wrong with the people in the cottage?"

"What do you mean, wrong?" Doc narrowed his eyes, peering at me. "How do you know there's anything wrong with them?" he added.

I told him about my two incidents with them, adding Alice's comments of the afternoon to the mix.

"Alice is a busybody at times." Doc did not look pleased. "I want you to stay away from them, Annie. People who rent here are entitled to their privacy. No snooping," he added.

"I wasn't snooping. I was just walking by. The racket inside sounded serious. I just wondered if I should do something about it," I defended myself.

"It's none of your business," Doc carefully enunciated each word of his last statement, making it absolutely clear to me that asking about taking measurements was useless. If anything was going to happen toward unraveling those mysteries, it would be up to Alice and me, and maybe Ty.

"Let's go for that walk, Annie," Ty came to the rescue, giving Doc a hard look.

"I'm sorry, Annie," offered Doc in a softer tone. "Just do as I ask. I know better. Have a good time, kids." With that, Doc left the kitchen to Ty and me.

Ty came over and gave me a hug. We stood there hugging and rocking. It felt so good. Phooey on the ghost, phooey on the neighbors. Darn it! Phooey on J, too. Why couldn't she just, for Pete's sake, take the week off like normal people?

Ty stroked my hair, and I nuzzled my face into his soft sweatshirt.

"Let's get out of here. We can talk about everything on the way to Ocean Beach. It's a long walk. I want to spend some time with you, Annie." Ty lifted my chin and looked at me. "Okay?"

The roller coaster started to the top. A sense of adventure and expectation replaced the disappointment of the day. I laughed, "Okay."

Chapter 11
THE CLUE AT OCEAN BEACH

"DOC GOT A LITTLE WEIRD this afternoon when we went to see the cops about the boat," Ty began as we headed along the surf toward Ocean Beach. "He got very preoccupied when he heard about the fingerprint match."

"Did you ask him what was wrong?" I began to think there was more to Doc then met the eye. *For instance,* I thought, *why is he so protective of the neighbors' privacy?*

"Yeah, I asked. He said he was just tired of having his boat messed with. What happened with Alice?" Ty inquired, pushing hair out of his eyes. The wind was whipping up out of the east, bringing in a bright haze of light fog off the ocean.

I told Ty about my discussion with her regarding the neighbors. We had started our walk with arms around each other's waists, but the walking was strenuous, and now we were holding hands.

"She's going over to the cottage one way or the other. If the Madonna Ghost shows up, she expects to follow her to the tunnel entrance. If not, she's going over around 1 AM to measure for the tunnel entrance, while everyone there is asleep. She hopes."

Ty pulled me close and kissed the top of my head saying, "I don't know if I like her doing that alone. What if they catch her? She's not exactly trained for guerrilla warfare or anything."

"We could meet her there," I suggested, touching my hair where Ty kissed me.

This is very hard, I thought. *Trying to think straight, when this boy you are crazy about keeps kissing you and hugging you takes a lot of concentration.*

"You heard Doc," Ty replied, oblivious of my struggle.

"But Alice didn't hear Doc, and I think you're right. Alice might need our help," I reasoned. "I promised her I would ask Doc about taking measurements and about looking into how legitimate these guys at the cottage are. She told me that if she couldn't get Doc to help, she'll do it herself."

"Let's call her when we get to Ocean Beach," Ty said. "Maybe she's changed her mind."

"You've known Alice for a long time, haven't you, Ty?"

"Since I was about six," he replied, looking at me with curiosity. "Why?"

"Do you think she's overreacting? Could this ghost thing have made us all a little too sensitive?"

"Alice is into this psychic stuff, but she likes to approach it with a scientific viewpoint. I think she wants to authenticate the ghost historically, not just have a ghost story to tell. She'd also like to prove that paranormal events do occur," he responded.

"So, you would rule out hysteria in her case? She isn't exaggerating her observations about the neighbors, because she has become high strung about the ghost?" I probed.

"Alice is never hysterical. She's out there with her ideas at times, because they fascinate her, not because she's unhinged," he concluded, filling in the details of my portrait of Alice.

"Think about your own experiences with the cottage people, Annie. Are you exaggerating because you're worried about J?" he asked.

"I don't think so, Ty. Let's try to lay out what we have to go on so far," I proposed as we came upon a telephone pole embedded in the sand. Having washed up in some previous storm, it made a nice seat. I picked up a stick and began to write in the sand.

"The ghost."

Ty followed my lead, adding, "Real or imagined?"

"All three of us saw it," I countered. "How could it be imagined? I wouldn't characterize any of us as that far out."

"The tunnel," Ty wrote.

"Trap door location," made number three.

I thought for a moment, and then added, "J's earring. I don't know what fits and what doesn't. Maybe if we lay it all out, we'll see a pattern. This is what J tells me cops do when they're working on a case."

"The disappearance of *Star*," was Ty's next entry.

He continued, "The neighbors."

I looked at Ty. "Do you think the neighbors know about the ghost? Could they be acting so crazy because they know about her?"

He shrugged. "Why would they be so defensive about a ghost?"

As he said the word "defensive," I thought of the cottage key in Doc's closet. Why was Doc so touchy about the neighbors?

A few minutes went by as we thought about our list, the surf creeping up closer to it with each wave.

At last, I added, "Where is J?"

"Do you think her absence is related to the ghost business or the neighbors?" Ty asked.

"I don't know. It's just another mystery." As we stared at the list, a wave licked hungrily at the last entry.

I got up, looking at the list and feeling helpless. Ty joined me, and we continued on our way along the beach. I glanced back. The list was almost gone, erased by the incoming tide.

By the time we reached Ocean Beach, the bright haze had been swept away and replaced by a gray cloud cover. The air was warm and the breeze brisk.

"I'm starved, Ty."

"Good," he replied, "because we are going on our first real date, Miss Tillery. I'm taking you out to dinner."

I smiled my pleasure at him and giggled. There I was, on that roller coaster again.

"I know a nice place right on the bay. We can sit on the porch and watch the sunset." Ty guided me off the beach to the maze of sidewalks that connected the homes on Ocean Beach.

Hand in hand, we made our way to the little restaurant. The air tempted my nostrils with whiffs of garlic, basil, tomatoes, and french fries. I was faint with hunger. We went inside, where a waiter led us to the open-air porch. The bay glistened despite the banks of gray clouds. Boats scurried for their moorings, as skippers and passengers sought land for the evening meal.

"I'll be right back, Annie," Ty announced and made his way back the way we came.

Good idea, I thought. Thinking he had gone to the restroom, I followed. When I returned to the table, he still wasn't back, but a basket of crusty warm bread and some butter awaited me. Ty returned as I started my second piece of bread.

"I called Alice," he declared. "She's relieved to have our support tonight."

"I hope your uncle's not too angry," I worried.

"I'll have to deal with that," Ty replied. "I can't let Alice do this alone. You don't have to go, Annie, if you're not comfortable. I don't want you to do it if you don't feel right about it. I don't always agree with Doc. We have butted horns in the past."

"No, Ty. I'll have to deal with your uncle, too. I'm less comfortable staying behind."

So, it was done. We would meet Alice at the designated time, and, I hoped, solve a few mysteries in doing so.

We ordered our meal, a spicy Mediterranean seafood stew with tons of French bread preceded by a huge fresh green salad.

Halfway through our meal, my hunger receding, I looked around me. The rustic little restaurant was just right for the setting. The porch was just an add-on room with half walls on three sides, providing all with a view of the bay. The unfinished wood gave off a resinous aroma, the sand on the floor adding just the right touch. I loved this first date. It was perfect.

I turned to share my thoughts with Ty and caught him watching me.

"Annie, will you write to me when I'm at school in September?"

"Will you come to visit me in New York when you're on break?" I countered.

We laughed, feeling joy and triumph in this happy-sounding future. Ty wiped my nose with his napkin. "Tomato sauce," he said.

The room grew brighter, drawing our attention to the scene outside. The sun had appeared through a break in the clouds. Shafts of light glanced off the bay, making pools of golden water. As if caught in the act of peering through the window, the sun disappeared, as the clouds drew together again.

"What a neat show for our first date, Ty."

"Yeah, it's a good omen to see a silver lining on the clouds."

The sun peeked in and out of the clouds for the next hour, each appearance different in its colors and moods. We finished dessert and Ty paid the bill. We left the restaurant, walking toward the ferry slip. The sidewalks were crowded on all sides by hotels, restaurants, shops, real estate offices, bakeries, and bars. Summer people sat on benches, eating ice cream cones, glowing with tans and rested psyches.

"There's a boat dock up past the ferry slip. We can sit there and watch the water traffic and the lights on Long Island for a while. It's too soon to go back." Ty guided me in that direction.

"Won't it take us a long time to walk back?" I asked, turning to look at him.

Ty was scanning the sky and sniffing at the breeze.

"It's getting nasty," he replied. "We'll take the water taxi back, okay?"

"Sure," I agreed as we turned from the sidewalk to the marina with its aisles of boat slips.

"Lot of people at the dock tonight," Ty observed. "Weather report must be bad."

I looked at the boats up and down the dock.

"Why do those powerboats have those tower things on top with all those gadgets? I don't know what to call them."

"Those are tuna towers with rigging for tuna fishing. The outriggers ..."

Ty's voice was drowned out by the deafening sound of a motor so powerful I could feel it vibrating up thorough my toes and into my chest. We turned to see the long menacing shape of a cigarette boat pull into a slip near the marina entrance to town. Two men held the boat onto the dock with a line, while a third leaped to the dock, holding a brown cardboard package.

We grabbed for each other, realizing that the man was from the cottage. Instinctively, we ducked behind the protruding bow of a nearby boat. The cigarette boat pulled away from the dock as quickly as it pulled in.

"Let's follow him," I hissed in Ty's ear. We ran to the marina entrance just in time to see the man walking quickly in the direction of the ferry slip. We raced to catch up, slowing only when we were close, hoping not to draw too much attention. My side hurt. This should not be done on a full stomach.

The neighbor headed directly for the crowd at the ferry dock. The last passengers were boarding the ferry, which would leave momentarily. Our friend tossed the package at a man on the lower deck of the ferry, laughing as the other man strained to catch it.

"Hey, watch it, sir," protested the ticket taker, who was a kid my age.

"Oh, sorry, just something he forgot to take back to the mainland with him." The neighbor saluted and headed back in our direction.

"I hope he doesn't recognize us, Ty," I gasped. He grabbed me, wrapping himself around me in a bear hug just as our quarry passed us. I opened the one eye that Ty didn't have covered and watched as the man went by. He was tossing a key chain in the air. As he did it a second time, something odd clicked off in my head. It was as if I knew his name and had just remembered it. But, it slipped away again just as quickly. He was gone. Ty stopped hugging me.

"Don't do that when I can't give my full attention to it," I said, pretending to be annoyed.

"Okay," Ty said amiably. "Now pay attention." This time he kissed me. The roller coaster slid down the dip and did two complete circles, turning me upside down. When he stopped, I didn't know which end was up.

"Did you pay attention this time, Annie?"

I pressed my lips together but couldn't think of a thing to say. I was busy checking my vital signs.

"Did you see where he went?" Ty asked.

"Yes, he's in the bar over there. Should we wait for him?"

"No, it's late. No one knows where we are. He might be in there all night. We need to be home in time to say good night to Doc."

Ty was right. The wind was whipping up choppy little white caps on the bay, and the breeze bore a damp uncomfortable mist.

"We better get going before they stop running the water taxis," Ty urged.

We got the taxi and settled into a low, wooden seat with ten other people. I was cold, snuggling closer to Ty. I put my hands in my sweatshirt pocket, hoping to draw away the chill. My fingers hit a tiny metallic object. Curiously, I pulled it out and recognized it immediately as the earring back I'd found last night in the tunnel.

All of a sudden, a thought hit me so powerfully that I started to stand, sucking in my breath.

"What's the matter, Annie?" Ty grasped my hand in alarm.

"I think this earring back belongs to J's earring. You know, the one I found outside the cottage," I searched his face to see if he understood my breathless fear.

"How can you be positive, Annie?" asked Ty. "Aren't they all the same?"

"I don't know for sure, Ty. I'll be able to tell when we get back to Windalee. It's just that I have this awful gut feeling about this. Why was J in the tunnel?"

I sat back as the water taxi started up, wishing we could instantly transport ourselves to my bedroom to see if the earring back matched the earring.

"Ty, did anything strike you as terribly familiar about our friend from the cigarette boat?"

"Umm, yup, from the first time I met him."

"Something about him keeps nagging at me. I wish I could put my finger on it."

Chapter 12

THE SNOOPS

WE RAN FROM THE FERRY slip, where the water taxi left us off, to Windalee. I had to find out if the earring back in my pocket fit J's earring.

"Have you got a magnifying glass?" I huffed out the words as I trotted along, trying to ignore the stitch in my side.

"Yeah, I'll go get the glass. I'll meet you in your room."

I ran into my room, skidding into the dresser. The earring rested in a small dish. As I tried to pick it up, my hands shook so badly that I decided to sit on the bed to catch my breath, not wanting to lose the earring.

Ty slammed the screen door, his quick footsteps making their way to my room.

"Does it fit?" he shot out as soon as he caught sight of me.

"I didn't try it yet. My hands were shaking too badly. Let's try it now."

Ty produced the magnifying glass. I stood up, placing the earring on the bedspread. Next, I fished the back out of my sweatshirt and placed it next to the earring. We knelt on the floor, leaning on the bed, like two children saying their bedtime prayers. The back fit perfectly on J's earring.

"Don't all earrings have the same size backs?"

I shook my head. "No, there's no standard size. Just because this fits doesn't mean it's a match either," I added. "That's why I need the glass. I know that the jeweler who made this earring makes a mark on all his pieces. It's a tiny crown."

Ty went to the bed stand to get the lamp. Removing the shade, he held it directly over me, as I studied the tiny piece of metal.

"I see it!" I whispered. "Oh, Ty, what are the chances of this earring back belonging to someone else? Look," I hissed, squinting through the glass.

I could see the jeweler's mark on the tiny piece of metal that now rested securely against the earring. We could also see a small ridge that was the length of the earring's post and how it fit into a corresponding groove in the earring's back.

I sat on the bed, panic burning its way up my neck and into my cheeks.

How had J lost her earring? Why in two different spots? My mouth went dry with the dread that now raced in my blood. Something was terribly wrong.

"Maybe we'll get some answers tonight," Ty offered, sitting down beside me, arms around me.

"I'm numb, Ty. I know something is wrong. J doesn't lose things. She would've called by now."

Nothing could stop me from trying to find out what was happening at the neighbors'. Everything pointed there: the ghost, the tunnel, and the earring. Determination put some steel into me. I couldn't give into my fear now. I must act.

"Let's go and do our charade for Doc," I said, handing the magnifying glass back to Ty.

Doc was in the kitchen in the main house, sitting at the kitchen table with some papers.

"What are you two up to tonight?" he asked, peering at us over his reading glasses.

"There's a movie we want to watch on TV," answered Ty.

"Well, lock up when you're done. I'm going to bed real soon." Doc returned to his paperwork.

Good, I thought, *we won't have to outwait him. It's 11:30. We'll be there in plenty of time to meet Alice.*

Ty turned on the TV, and we spent an agonizing fifteen minutes watching a vintage sci-fi thriller about aliens taking over the African violets in Brazil. Doc went to bed, clucking and shaking his head over our choice of movie.

At 12:30 AM, Doc's light went out. We left a night-light on in my hallway, and Ty stuffed some pillows in his bed to make it look slept in. We closed up the house. "It's a good thing Merlin sleeps with Doc," I whispered.

Ty threw a dark sweatshirt to me and put one on himself. "Camouflage," was his one-word explanation. We left Windalee by hugging the building and shrubs where possible.

We slipped into the shadows of the wind-whipped pines bordering the boardwalk, melting away like maple sugar candy in the rain. My heart thudded in my ears.

"Ty, are you sure we're doing the right thing?" I whispered.

"Too late to think about that now. Alice will be waiting for us. You're not getting cold feet are you?" he quipped.

"No, not me. I was just testing you," came my reply, made flip by the exhilaration that went with my fear.

We could barely see the familiar curve in the boardwalk up ahead that signaled our nearness to the cottage.

"Let's get off the boardwalk here and find a place to wait for Alice where we can't be seen," I said.

"I like the way you think, Miss Annie," replied Ty. "We can also get out of this wind. I hope we're done here before this storm hits, or we'll be soaked." Jumping down into the dunes, he reached up to help me down.

Hunkering down into a hollow, we made ourselves comfortable in a spot where we could watch the traffic coming from both directions. We also had a good view of the front of the cottage.

I looked at my watch. I was 12:50. Alice would be along in the next fifteen minutes—if all went well. I wondered if she had been able to make the measurements to determine where our tunnel came up in relation to Madonna Ghost's disappearing act.

"My leg's falling asleep," Ty complained. Minutes ticked by. It was 1:15. No Alice.

"Where is she?" I hissed into Ty's ear. He replied, "I'm going to look around a bit. You stay here. She may be holed up the same way we are, close by."

Before I could protest, he was gone. This experience was really teaching me what wired meant. When Ty finally showed up three minutes later, I felt like screaming.

"No sign of her," he breathed as he settled down into our hidey-hole again. "Something must have held her up."

"Or, she decided not to show." Another thought occurred to me.

"I hoped nothing happened to her, Ty."

"Me too. But sitting here isn't helping anything. Let's take a look at the neighbors."

"Shhh," I hissed into Ty's ear. Footsteps approached on the boardwalk. We huddled together, trying our best not to be seen. The footsteps receded, their rhythm faintly familiar.

"Who was that?" I whispered.

"Don't know. But they're gone now," Ty replied, grabbing my hand.

We got out of our hideout, trying to keep our heads below the level of the boardwalk until we could see that the coast was clear. It was very quiet. Even the wind made just a small humming sound here in the protection of the trees. The hairs on the back of my neck prickled.

We stepped up onto the wall and crossed it. In two seconds, we were in the cottage yard. The cottage nestled in its hollow like a great sleeping bear, dark, silent, and still. Ty grabbed my hand, pointed to the window nearest us, and then made a sweeping gesture encompassing the building. I nodded, realizing that he wanted us to check the windows. I nodded again.

Something kept nagging at me. My brain was screening the environment and coming up with a red warning light, but I couldn't figure out which system was feeding in the sensitive information. I chalked it up to not being cut out to be a snoop.

The first two sides of the house offered breaking and entering as the only possible way for us to get any idea of what was inside.

As we rounded the corner to the third side, a gleam of light shone from a crack alongside one window. Creeping up to the window, I knew what was wrong. There were no crickets, no toads, no normal sounds at all. The loudest noise was the crashing of the surf, whipped by a considerable wind, on the beach below us. The light was coming through a space where the window shade didn't quite meet the side of the window. We both peered in, Ty above me. There was a large bundle on the floor. No, it was a person. What an odd position for that person to be sleeping in.

They were asleep, weren't they? Oh, I see. Their hands were tied behind their back. The hands. The shape of the head. My mind grasped it all at last. We had found J. She was tied up on the cottage floor. I opened my mouth to call out to her and was about to throw myself against the window when something swooshed beside me.

I felt myself lifted off my feet by a strong arm, grabbing me from behind.

"Oh, no …" A hand clamped over my mouth.

"Struggle, you bitch, and I'll put you away," growled my captor. I went limp. From the side of my eye, I could see Ty slung over the big burly neighbor's shoulder, dark hair lank across his face.

"We're going to walk to the marina to get the boat," my captor continued. "You're going to walk on your own, and you're going to remember that I'll blow your brains out after I make you watch me do the same for Prince Charming here if you make a false move."

I nodded, thinking that I must try to remember every detail about this man. Aunt J drilled that into my head.

"If ever anyone tries anything funny with you, Annie, try to remember every detail about them."

A picture of J on the floor of the cottage filled my mind. *I must get out of this to go back and help her,* I thought.

The other captor dropped Ty on the sand, as he began to stir. He rolled on his back and looked up at me. I shook my head.

"Get up," my captor barked at Ty. "And don't try anything, or your girlfriend's brains will get splattered all over this beach."

Ty got to his feet, and our captor bound our hands behind our backs.

"Start walking west," the other captor growled. It was the man we had seen delivering the package to the ferry earlier in the evening.

My captor was only a few inches taller than I. He was very muscular, with long dark hair. I couldn't see his face. He had a tattoo on his left arm, but I couldn't see its design in the dark. I wasn't even sure it was a tattoo. The other one was tall. He wasn't American, at least not born here. His English was good, but his accent was very pronounced. It also didn't sound like he had learned English in this country.

My captor was a New Yorker, the accent as familiar as the back of my hand.

We walked rapidly, the wind lashing us, rain beginning to pelt us in fits and starts. The surf pounded, and now, lightning split the sky in the west.

My mind raced from one means of escape to another. We had no chance here on the beach. The noise of the surf would drown out even gunshots. The marina might give us a better chance. Someone might have gone down to check on their boat before the storm. There was no choice but to trudge ahead and keep alert.

Finally, we were at the marina. There was no one. Not even a seagull. In a few short minutes, we were aboard *Star*.

"You're going to sail us to the mainland, kids. No funny stuff. I do know how to sail, but I can't do it and watch you, too." As he said this, he dropped his key chain to the floor. It was J's key chain! That was what had bothered me about him earlier this evening. The key chain was what I had recognized. For some reason, this made me madder than anything.

"What are you going to do with my aunt?" I couldn't hold back anymore.

He looked blank.

"The woman who's tied up at the cottage," I filled in.

"Her?" laughed "Tattoo." "After tonight, she'll be a nice match for her dental records when they sift through the ashes. That's the price for snooping where you don't belong."

Maybe it wasn't Aunt J I saw. This couldn't be real. I thought about just getting up and excusing myself to go back to Windalee and get some sleep.

"What is it with you guys? Why do you have my aunt?"

"She knows too much about us now. She could blow our chances to do what we came here for. We have big plans to deal with your government." Our captors were getting impatient.

"My government?" Ty nearly exploded. "Aren't you Americans? What's your problem?" We were both clearly stalling for time.

Tattoo sneered, wiping his nose on his wrist, the one with the gun. If only I could grab it.

"We're American in name only, so we can rent houses and cars and not be questioned about other business transactions. It makes it easier for us to get the things we need."

"Need! To do what?" Ty demanded.

"Your government has imprisoned some of our brothers, whose only crime is that they worked for the liberation of our country. We act on their behalf."

"Tall One" kept getting in Ty's face, taunting him finally with, "Do I look familiar to you?"

"Yeah, vaguely. But, I bet we move in different circles," Ty shot back.

"Not so different. You know my father."

Ty gave Tall One a hard look. "What are you talking about?"

With obvious satisfaction, Tall One continued. "Yes. Professor Taled. You took his Philosophies of the Middle East course. You used to attend seminars in our home."

Ty's eyes narrowed, as he tried to put this all together. "That's it. Your picture was on his desk. That's why you never would speak to me at the cottage. Your buddy here always came to the door."

"Bingo!" Tall One had a talent for sarcasm.

"I certainly got his point about the flourishing early civilizations of the Middle East, but he didn't seem like a terrorist."

"Oh, he is not. Nor is my brother. They are the reason why our cause is not taken seriously. They don't fight for it. I see things differently. I believe change can only come from violence. Violence makes the necessary point."

"Your father is a peaceful man. This is going to kill him." Ty shook his head.

"Someday, he will see it my way." Tall One seemed confident of something we could not grasp.

Tattoo joined in, getting more agitated. "We will get your government's attention with what we are planning, and our brothers, one of whom is my real brother, will be free to carry on the fight!"

"But our government—" I started.

"Shut up!" Tattoo screamed, kicking the back of my knees to make me fall.

Ty lunged for him and got the same treatment for his efforts. We struggled to our feet, spitting sand from our mouths and moved toward *Star*, aided by another push.

"You can't sail this boat in this storm," Ty broke in. "It's too dangerous."

"I don't think you have a real handle on what dangerous is, kid. Just shut up and let's get going. No engine, please!"

Tall One cast off the lines, and we blew out of the slip, bumping the pilings as we went. The last bump put an idea in my head. When we got out into the bay, maybe we could knock one of these guys overboard. I had to get back to J.

"You'll never get away with killing my aunt. She's a cop." I needed to get them to talk. I kept thinking the more information I could get out of them, the more ideas I could get on how to get away from them. Maybe in time to save J.

"She was snooping where she didn't belong. We know she's a cop. She won't be the first dead cop either."

Tall One piped in. "She knows too much about our operation. We can't afford to have supplies cut off to our people in the bomb factories …"

The buzzing in my head kept me from hearing the rest of the conversation.

Bomb factories! I was stunned by the revelation. They were going to make their words about violence a reality. They were terrorists! The vague feeling of unreality was no longer vague, as these thoughts formed and sunk in. Gradually, I realized that they would never let Ty and me live either. Our only chance was to lose them somehow out in the bay.

Ty yelled from the helm, "If you don't want to use the engine, somebody's gotta raise the main."

The short guy poked me. "Help your boyfriend. No funny stuff."

I jerked my arm away. "He has to tell me what to do. I never sailed before." Before he could say anything, I passed Ty on my way to the mast. He gestured up toward the mast. "Just pull with all your might, and cleat the halyard when you're done," he smiled.

What the hell is he smiling about? I thought, pulling loose the sail cover and shock cord that held the mainsail in place. I wrapped the halyard around the winch and began to pull. With the sail about a third of the way up, I realized that I was completely enveloped in the wildly flapping sail. I hung my full weight on the halyard, and soon I was flapping around the mast with the sail. *Ty is doing this on purpose,* I thought.

As this revelation occurred to me, Ty appeared in the folds of the sail, making motions to untangle me and the halyard. The noise was deafening as the wind howled, the sail flapped, and the metal fittings on the sail and halyard rapped into the aluminum mast. Ty looked at me hard and said, "Our only chance is if I go out there under full sail. In this wind, that'll capsize the boat. Hopefully, it'll sink, and we can swim to shore. Keep a boat cushion close at all times, and use it as a life preserver. They'll never let us wear vests. Just keep watching me. It's our only chance."

Suddenly, the sail went up as one of our captors accidentally turned the boat in the right direction. "What a jerk," Ty mouthed at me.

We made our way back to the cockpit and took over.

"Annie, take the helm and head it to 270° when I get up to the headstay to raise the genny."

We did a precision job. Ty ran along the deck, holding onto the lifelines, and took over the helm. "Hold on tight," he said to all in the cockpit. Our two captors just leveled their guns more diligently at us.

Ty fell off the wind, and *Star* dug in. Every line strained. The boat creaked ominously, and the wind began to sing and hum across the sail. Everyone braced, as the boat heeled obliquely to starboard.

We continued on this way, catching gusts every few minutes that sent the starboard gunwales awash for a minute or two. Lines were thrumming with the strain. I watched the sheet on the genny begin to fray, and the winches slipped a few inches.

We were soaked, the lights of Fire Island had been lost in about three minutes, and the lights on Long Island were beyond our visibility in the rainy black curtains that stretched out in front of us. I don't remember breathing. Every so often, I clutched at our boat cushions.

I stared and stared, hoping to see a light from the shore. Some place to swim toward when the storm finally spilled us into the water.

Chapter 13
THE STORM

I WATCHED THE LAST STRANDS of the jib sheet twirl free.

The large sail seemed to move away from me at warp nine and stopped with a loud snap in the murky, fog-shrouded area of the bow. *Star* tipped back to port with the sudden release of wind from that sail, catching our captor off guard. Ty steered even farther off the wind. The boat heeled again to starboard, launching Mutt and Jeff off balance again.

With the genny gone from the starboard side of the boat, I had an unobstructed view out of the cockpit. I thought I saw a light twinkling in the distance, but it could be just the rain or lightning. No, there it was again. It appeared to be stationary. I could tell that Ty saw it, too. He looked at me. Our captors had regained their seating and now had a gun planted in Ty's side.

Just then a gust caught the main full, and the head stay snapped, an incredible vibrating sound that I could feel resonate in my spine. The mast swayed and, in slow motion, appeared to be falling toward us. Lightning flashed, and a second gust, worse than the first, slammed the main. The mast popped out of its mounting and went over the starboard side. We all stared in wonder.

Star struggled forward under the weight of the two dragging sails.

Now I could see many twinkling lights. We were very close to shore. So much for sinking the boat in the middle of the bay. Ty was battling the tiller. I got up to help him. The cockpit floor went out from under me, and my world lit up in flashing lights as my head cracked into the cabin bulkhead. The last thing I saw was the pistol coming down on Ty's head.

The light show subsided, as the pelting rain and the water in the cockpit splashed me back to reality. I pulled myself up, fighting the nausea from my cracked head. Ty lay ashen-faced across the gunwale. But our captors were gone. Water was washing over the port side, and I screamed, "Ty, wake up, the boat's sinking!"

I splashed water into his face, finally rousing him. Sitting bolt upright, he grunted his satisfaction. Terror brought him back to reality fast. "We can't sink, Annie. I know this place. We're right off an old fishing dock. I think we hit a submerged piling. But look. See how that cable on the starboard side is straining? We're hung up on something. *Star's* not going anywhere. We'll have to swim to shore. Take a boat cushion. The wind and waves will wash us up on the dock. Doc's going to kill me. Look at *Star*."

"Oh really, Ty. It seems like Doc will have to stand in line with those who've been out to get us today. I can't believe those guys didn't shoot us."

"I guess they thought we'd drown because the boat would sink before we regained consciousness. Let's get the police. Maybe we can still help," he said, helping me into the water. My spirits soared, as we climbed onto the dock and saw the pay phone at the end of a rutted parking lot.

"911," Ty screamed into the phone.

I grabbed the phone. "Please, my aunt," I cried, finally breaking down. "She's tied up. They're going to burn the house. Please warn them."

Ty retrieved the phone. He told them who we were. He gave them Doc's name and number on the island. He told them about J. After a few seconds, he handed me the phone. "Do you have her shield number or something?"

I took the phone and gave them enough information to get J into a meeting of the Joint Chiefs of Staff at the Pentagon. I told them how we had seen J through the window while snooping around the cottage, and how we had been kidnapped but escaped.

"Stand by, Miss Tillery. Now that the wind is dying, Suffolk County Police is deploying a helicopter to pick you up. We already got an all points out from Mr. Egan. Just sit tight."

I hadn't noticed, but the rain had stopped, the wind had died, and a few stars appeared between holes in the clouds. I was numb to all sensation but the obsession to save J.

At last the whomp-whomp-whomp of the copter's rotor barely preceded the blinding light of its strobe. The craft picked out the parking lot, landed, and scooped us aboard. The shore slipped away, and I caught a glimpse of *Star*, a mass of cables, torn sails, and lines.

As we approached Fire Island, I saw the bright orange glow of a fire. I screamed, and Ty grabbed me. "We're too late," I began to scream, "J's in there." Desolation claimed me. I had failed.

"Maybe not. Maybe she got out." Ty comforted lamely.

The helicopter barely set down on the ferry dock, letting us race away from the rotors to the small group of waiting figures. As we came closer to them, a familiar form took shape.

"Lt. Red," I sobbed. "J, J is in the fire. Please help me save her," I cried as I tugged at him.

His big hands grasped me by the shoulders. "Annie, we got her out. She's been airlifted to Good Samaritan Hospital. She's alive!"

I sat on the ground, sobbing my relief. Someone placed a jacket around my shoulders. I heard soft conversation behind me, but I couldn't make out what they were saying.

"Will she be okay?" I dared to ask, panic locking into my heart again.

"We hope so, Annie. We're waiting for the police boat to take us over to the hospital now."

"How did you find her?" I asked, beginning to realize that I must be missing whole parts of what had happened to save J.

"We'll try to fill you in on the way over. Your dad's going to meet us at the hospital," said Red.

Ty put his arm around me, as I looked from one serious face to another. This time, I couldn't muster the courage to ask again if J would be okay.

Chapter 14
The Neighbors' Secret

"Here's some hot chocolate," one of the Suffolk County police officers said. "You both could use the emergency room yourselves," she added. A paramedic appeared from somewhere and was dressing Ty's head wounds. "You've got a concussion there, buddy. That's my guess." She handed me an ice pack and said, "Put that on your forehead. We'll try to get the swelling down." I began to cry again, shaking involuntarily so that the chocolate spilled out of the cup.

"Where's Alice?" I blurted out, suddenly remembering that she had never shown up.

"She's gone to the hospital, as well," offered Doc.

The bad guys seemed to have tried to wipe us all out, I thought, shivering. In spite of myself, my curiosity took over. I began to question Doc. Red went off to see about the boat.

"What happened to her?" I pressed.

"Alice got to the cottage early for your snooping expedition," Doc explained, leveling an accusatory gaze at us. I looked down at my hot chocolate, sheepishly.

"C'mon, Doc," Ty added weakly. "Where'd this situation be if we hadn't decided to snoop?"

"Perhaps there'd be fewer casualties if you had come to me," he added sternly.

"But you kept putting us off the neighbors," Ty protested. "We didn't think you'd listen."

"What happened to Alice?" I persisted, trying to get past this uncomfortable little exchange.

"She saw Jill through the window at the cottage, just as you did," Doc began.

"How did you know that we saw her?" I interrupted.

"You told the police, and they filled us in while you were flying over here. I've been in constant contact with them since Alice filled me in. Anyway, she recognized Jill and started back to Glass House to call me. I don't know why she didn't come straight to Windalee," he mused. "Maybe she thought she might run into the neighbors. She told me they were gone when she saw Jill through the window."

"Why didn't she get Jill out then?" I demanded.

"Alice is no dope, Annie. She had no way of knowing whether your friends would come back while she was inside," Doc chided.

"On her way home, she caught her foot in a hole in the boardwalk near Glass House. Her ankle's either badly sprained or broken. She crawled to her house and called me. I set out for the cottage."

A light went off in my head. The footsteps? They were so familiar, because they were Doc's. He limps.

"As I left Windalee, I saw two rather bulky bodies slipping onto the property around the cottage. I decided to call Lt. Red and your dad first and then head out the Glass House."

"Why my father?" I probed.

"Your father knew about your aunt's undercover work here on the island. In fact, it was a tip from him that put us onto the neighbors."

"What undercover work?" I demanded, feeling confused, like I had come in on the wrong story.

Lt. Red walked up to us at that point. Helping me to my feet, he urged us on, "Boat's here, folks. Let's go."

Under heavy protest, Ty had been put on a stretcher while I was speaking with Doc. With a mixture of anticipation and dread, I shook off momentary dizziness and tried to steady my feet as we rushed toward the police launch.

"Lt. Red, what undercover work was Jill doing? Why didn't someone tell me?"

"If someone told you, Annie, it wouldn't be undercover work," he answered, slipping an arm around me. "It's what she does, Anne Tillery. Usually, she's well protected. This time we underestimated the enemy."

"You still haven't told me what she was doing," I complained.

"The men who captured her are members of a terrorist group. They receive shipments of raw material here on the island for a bomb factory in the city. She was posing as a contact between the guys in the cottage and the supplier of explosives."

My head seemed to clear as things fell into place. "Yeah, the two creeps on the boat said that J knew about a bomb factory." I buried my head in his big shoulder. "She could've died," I sobbed. "Why does she do this dangerous stuff?" I asked, mostly to myself. Knowing the answer, I jerked my head up to look into his eyes, "She is going to live, isn't she?" I begged.

Lt. Red tightened his grip on me and replied, "We'll see in a few minutes."

The launch punched its way across the choppy bay, still churned up by the backwash from the storm. A cruiser was waiting on the other side. I felt like I was watching the whole drama from somewhere outside myself.

Ty was whisked off toward an emergency room, as Doc, Lt. Red, and I looked for information.

"ICU is down that corridor and to your right."

Lt. Red pushed open the double doors of the Intensive Care Unit. The nurse's station occupied the center of the dimly lit area, an island of lights. Nurses alternated their gazes between paperwork and a bank of beeping monitors that flashed numbers and wavy lines at them.

Lt. Red offered his badge and said Jill's name gruffly. *Get a grip*, I said to myself. *This is no time to faint*, I thought. As the light in the room dimmed and brightened, my mind tried desperately to reject where my body was taking it.

"Lt. Tillery's breathing on her own now," the efficient voice behind the desk reported. I suppressed the urge to ask who was doing it for her before, as the importance of that last statement sank in. I looked from

Lt. Red to the nurse to see if I had really heard what she had said. Her look was confident, comforting. He smiled broadly, squeezing me. I found my voice at last. "Where is she?"

"I'm here," came a weak, hoarse J from a cubicle on the left.

"What took you so long, Annie?" she teased. Despite her remark, she looked awful. Lips cracked, hair lank, bruises under her eyes.

"You're grounded, J. That's it! No more excuses. No more chances," I joked to keep from crying in front of her.

"It's okay, Annie. I'm going to make it, according to these nice people."

"You look like hell, J. Just because you're a cop doesn't mean you should look like one." I bit my lip as my attempt at a smile failed.

J started to choke and cough. The nurse rushed over and made her breathe from some contraption that helped clear her lungs. We looked on with concern as J's normal color returned.

"It's best if you leave now. When you come back tomorrow, she'll be much better," admonished the nurse.

I kissed J on the forehead. She squeezed my hand.

"Hang in there, chubby," she croaked. I smiled at the nickname from my seemingly long ago childhood. We left.

"Where's my dad?" I said into the air. Lt. Red and Doc were on the phone at the nurse's station. Finishing their phone calls, the two men gestured for me to follow them as we left the ward. A police officer had taken a station in front of the ICU. No chances were taken anymore.

"Where are we going?" I was beginning to get tired of never knowing where I was going.

"We can go get Ty and Alice in emergency. They're all glued together. Your dad is tied up with some people at the State Department. He's helping to compile some material that we'll use to identify the terrorists. He'll bring it out to us tomorrow."

"I bet the creeps set the fire to burn up some incriminating evidence as well as J," I muttered.

"We're in luck there, too," replied Doc. "The fire was put out before it consumed the whole cottage. Thanks to Alice."

With that said, we entered the emergency room by virtue of Lt. Red's badge. The star of that last comment was propped up in a wheelchair, a cast halfway up her thigh, a look of disgust on her face.

Ty was walking around with the help of an orderly.

"We've decided to keep young Mr. Egan overnight," the nurse responded to Doc's concerned look. "He has a mild concussion. We want to keep an eye on him."

I knelt beside Alice's wheelchair and gave her a kiss.

"Thank you. I will never be able to tell you how grateful I am. If it weren't for you, J would be dead. Maybe even Ty, too."

Her eyes filled up, and I started to cry again. I felt Ty's hand on my shoulder and rose to hug him. "I love you," I whispered in his ear. We held each other for a long moment, savoring the fact that we were alive to hug. I wasn't sure living would be so much fun when the powers that be realized what we had done this evening.

Doc wheeled Alice toward the exit, as Lt. Red gently pried me away from Ty. "Let's get you some rest," he urged with a husky voice. I didn't resist.

Chapter 15
THE TALE IS TOLD

STAR WAS RIDING THE CREST of a huge wave. We were just about to descend into the trough when Ty yelled for me to stop the boat. He had to put the mast back in place. The sail kept hitting me in the face, as I tried to apply the brakes. The sail was wet. Now, the sail was barking. No, it was Merlin.

I opened my eyes. I was in a strange bedroom with the little Scottish terrier tugging at my sheets. He seemed to be saying, "Get up, sleepyhead." Memory returned as I looked around. It hurt to open my eyes. I touched my forehead. Ouch. I tried to get out of bed. Every muscle resisted. Where was everybody? Where was I?

A soft knock came at the door. Doc's voice joined the knock. "How do you feel, Annie? Would you like some breakfast?"

"Yes, please." *I'm starving*, I realized. "I want to take a shower first, though."

Half an hour later, I was seated in the kitchen with a cup of Doc's excellent coffee. "When is Ty coming home?" I asked.

"I called the hospital this morning. They're waiting for the neurologist to look at the CAT scan. Then, they'll probably send him home."

"Well, good morning, fellow snoop." I spun around to see Alice wheeling herself into the kitchen from the porch.

"I stayed here in Doc's hospital last night," she explained.

"How's your ankle?"

"Oh, it's broken. I'm just grateful that Doc was able to get to your aunt before the flames did. When I called him, I passed out from the pain before I could tell him about someone being tied up on the floor in the cottage."

"She said, 'cottage,' and then nothing. I just made it to Glass House as fast as I could," Doc added.

"When he got there, I told him what I had seen. I had no idea that those scoundrels planned to set the place on fire, with someone in it, no less."

"I called the police and then ran back to the cottage," Doc continued.

"Weren't you afraid that the neighbors would be there?"

"I didn't have time. I also brought a pistol. A remnant from my working days. As I reached the cottage, I smelled smoke and could see flames through the front window. I threw a lawn chair through the window and pulled J out. I had to call the fire department. Fire is an enormous problem here. Everything is made of wood. Fire spreads easily because of the wind."

"One story has it that Fire Island got its name for the number of times every building in the small settlements burned to the ground," said Alice.

"Those small fire phones along the boardwalk really came in handy. The fire department was there in minutes with the paramedics for J. The police came next. I was able to get Lt. Red through them. You know the rest." Doc looked at me at the end of his story.

I shivered in spite of the warmth of the day. "You must have just missed seeing Ty and me being dragged off by our two friends. I wonder what happened to them. Any chance they'll be caught?" I looked up at Doc for an answer.

"Red tells me that J had a tiny transmitter so the police could trace her. When she didn't call in, but the location changed from Fire Island to Bay Shore and into the city twice, they became suspicious and sent someone out to check on the transmitter's location. They caught up with it in Brooklyn."

"What's in Brooklyn? Why was J there?" I asked.

"That's just it. When they located the transmitter, J wasn't there. The surveillance team got a picture of three men who came and went from the Brooklyn address."

I looked at Doc, confused.

Alice piped in, "They already had J as a prisoner. Doc's been filling me in," she explained.

Doc went on, "They continued to follow the signal. Last evening it was traced to a man who transferred a package to someone on the Ocean Beach ferry."

"The key chain," I yelled. "Was the transmitter in a key chain?" Of course, the man Ty and I spotted on the ferry dock last night. He had J's key chain, the key chain I had finally recognized later, while they held us captive on *Star*.

"How did you know about the transmitter?" Doc asked surprised.

"I didn't. I just figured it out," and I recounted what had happened to Ty and me in Ocean Beach the long ago time that was the previous night.

"Hello, Doc, it's Randy," came a call from the back door.

My father's head and familiar form were outlined in the screen door. I dropped the spoon I was holding. It clattered to the floor, giving me time to get my feelings under control. The old anger, the relief because my dad had shown up, the anxiety about a confrontation I knew we must have, all clamored to be first.

He and Doc shook hands. Alice was introduced. He looked at me for an instant and then came across the room, enveloping me in his strong arms, the familiar scent of his cologne filling my head and heart with my dad. The tears stung my eyes and prickled my nose, as I fought them back behind the iron gate I thought I had built to keep them in.

I heard Alice in the background. "Doc, wheel me outside. It's such a glorious day."

Randall released me. Holding me at arm's length, he scrutinized my face.

"You're never going to learn to pick on somebody your own size, are you?" he kidded.

More sternly, he added, "Why didn't you return my call, Annie?"

Here it comes, I thought. My head started to ache dully. "Because I didn't want to talk to you, Dad," I replied simply. "Your calls always make me feel guilty. I should call you. I should call Mom." I tried to ignore his hurt look.

He sat back on his heels, looking up at me, his face unreadable to me.

"You're not part of my life. You're always away. I really don't know my mother anymore."

"How can I be a part of your life, Annie, if you don't return my calls and talk to me? How can you know your mother unless you talk to her?"

"Oh, come on, Dad. Talking to Mom for most of my life has been like talking to a wall." That phrase again. "Nice house, nobody home," I shot back, feeling worse with every word.

"She needs us, Annie. Being in rehab hasn't been easy on her, either," he said more softly than I'd expected to hear.

"I needed her, too. I needed you. You're always away when there's a crisis, Dad," I accused. "J is there for me. She's my family." I choked on the last words. The thought that I had almost lost J flooded over me. I couldn't stop shaking.

Dad put his arms around me again. "I know you can't change your job. And I know Mom can't help it that she's an alcoholic. But, don't ask me to depend on either one of you, because I can't. I was on vacation here, with J. I didn't want to think about what having a vacation with my dad and mom, or even just my dad, would be like. So, Dad, I didn't return your call."

After a small silence, he said, "I don't know what to say to you, Annie. I can't argue with what you feel. But, I want you to know that I care intensely about you. I have offered you vacations with me. You've made other choices. I feel that you've made yourself as scarce as you claim I do."

He sighed, "If you want me to back off completely, I'll stop calling. I'll keep up with your life through Jill." His eyes bore into my face. They seemed to be the only part of him that hadn't slumped with his last comments. Could I have reached him somehow? A small flutter of panic at losing touch with him tugged at me. "I want you to let me call you at first, Dad. When I want to. I don't want to talk about Mom. I'll tell you when I do." I felt like a kidnapper making ransom demands.

"You won't know where to call me," he replied dully.

"J will tell me. You can tell her."

"I don't think you'll call," he resigned himself.

"I'll never know if I want to, Dad, unless you let me have the chance to feel like I want to."

I shuddered, thinking of all those times I had to come to the phone. I had to listen to that faraway voice, so familiar, so unreachable. I knew that we had to try it some different way.

"Okay, Annie," he said after a time. "I love you, girl. Don't you forget that."

Our eyes met for a moment, feelings made skittish with our history of hurt. He rose to his feet.

"Dad?" He looked back at me. "I'm glad you came, and I'm glad we talked." It was all I could manage. He nodded.

We became conscious of a new voice from the porch, where Alice and Doc had fled.

"That's Lt. Red." I jumped up to see if he had news for us.

"Come along, you two," Alice directed. "This nice gentleman has just returned from the cottage with a report on the crime scene."

Alice sounded different, somehow. I looked at her. She was giving Lt. Red her most charming smile, and he was enjoying every minute of it.

"The boys from Suffolk County Crime Scene have a good bit of evidence from the cottage," Lt. Red boomed. "Annie, you're looking better," he added.

"I may have something to add to the evidence myself," said Doc. "I'm waiting for a phone call from my old friends at the 'farm'; er, the CIA."

The phone rang. Doc went to answer it, his slight limp clearly resonating on the wood floors. He picked up the phone, his voice an intermittent unintelligible drone. I thought about the limp. It had popped up so unexpectedly last night. I had almost begun to suspect Doc of having some kind of connection with the neighbors.

"That was the hospital," was his welcome announcement when he returned to the porch. "We can pick up Ty and Jill anytime. In fact, Ty has already threatened to walk out."

"Let's go!" I yelled. "Come on, Dad." A jubilation unknown since I first set eyes on Ty filled me, as I rushed for the door, dragging Dad by the hand.

Chapter 16

HOMECOMING

TY WAS BACK TO HIS old self, except for his head bandages. J was walking on her own but still looked weak. Her hands shook, and she was sporting a cast on her left arm, broken when she was first captured.

When we arrived back at Windalee, the police were waiting for us. "Mr. Egan, will you come down to your boat with us? We want to free her from the piling she's hung up on and take her to the marina where we can look her over."

"Go ahead, Doc. I'll take care of J and Alice and Ty." Randall took J by the arm to direct her toward her room.

"Whoa!" she said. "I'll take the couch here. Alice and I will man the phones. Thank you very much." We laughed with pleasure at hearing J's bossy response.

"Thanks, but forget it, Mr. Tillery. I'm great, and I'm going with my uncle," asserted Ty.

Randall looked around him and shrugged at his failed attempt to play Florence Nightingale.

"Lt. Tillery, we need to get a statement from you. So, one of my detectives will take it now, if you don't mind," said one of the crime scene detectives. "And, are you Randall Tillery?" At a nod, he added, "I need one from you, too, sir."

We left the three of them behind with the detective and set off for the marina. The police launch took us across the now peaceful bay where *Star* rode her makeshift mooring. She had fared worse than the rest of us. Doc jumped from the launch onto her gently bobbing deck. He seemed to be comforting an old friend, as he made his way from one injury to another. "Lieutenant., I want to get her into the marina as soon as I can. Are you sending a rescue boat that can tow her, or shall I call my shipyard?" he called across to the dock.

"Our boat is coming," came the reply. "We need to determine just where she's wrapped onto the pilings."

I could see the bottom of the bay when I looked into the water. That's how shallow it was. There was a lot of eel grass undulating in the current, a few beer cans, and an odd-shaped mass glinting in the light.

"Detective, do you know where my aunt's transmitter is?" I couldn't remember if they had told me or not.

"Yes, Miss Tillery, it's here with the boat."

"Is that the key ring there on the bay bottom?" We both squinted at the object I had seen. The detective produced a boat hook and snatched the object off the floor of the bay. Sure enough, there were J's keys and the infamous key ring.

"Too bad those creeps didn't take the key ring last night. You'd know where they are now." I felt glum about them getting away.

"Can I have the key ring?" I asked, grabbing for it. The detective grabbed my wrist before I could touch the key ring.

"We're going to try for prints," he explained his action.

"Right," I replied, embarrassed.

The others had located the line that had *Star* stranded on the piling. They were trying to untangle some of the cables and lines when the rescue boat chugged alongside.

The police launch pulled back to a safe distance, enabling us to watch as *Star* was secured to the rescue boat, her mast lashed on deck, freed from the piling, and towed away. Doc stayed on *Star* to see her safely into the marina. Ty returned to me on the launch.

"Both of you will have to make a formal statement, even though you've told us what happened already," the detective told us. "We want you to try to remember everything you can. We'll get back to you in a couple of days." With this, he let us off at the marina, and we walked back to Windalee, enjoying the first few quiet moments we'd had in a while.

"I have one helluva headache," complained Ty.

"I feel like someone beat me with sticks," I added.

"You thinking of becoming a detective like your aunt, Annie?" asked Ty, wincing as he adjusted his bandage.

"Oh, right!" I said, letting go of his hand. "Me? If I never see another cop, I won't die," I ranted on. "I'm going to school to become a research scientist. I'll spend my life safely locked in a lab somewhere. This stuff is crazy. Your uncle's house looks like a scene from one of those emergency room TV shows with all these casualties."

He just looked at me as I waved my hands in the air. "I was almost shot, drowned. They could've thrown us in the house and set us all on fire."

Ty put his hand over his mouth. Was that a laugh he was covering? Dare he laugh at this situation.

"That's it. J's going to retire. She can open a bed and breakfast in Connecticut. She can sell strawberry jam at a roadside stand."

He was laughing out loud now. I stopped, and he hugged me, as I tried to figure out what was so funny. Finally, he managed to say, "Do they make granny aprons with holsters?" I didn't think it was funny.

I always worried, but J had never been hurt before. I was scared.

Windalee was indeed the home of the injured and lame. By 4 PM, Doc returned with a bandaged hand, sliced open by the sharp edge on *Star's* mast. Alice and J had managed to heat up a kettle with soup that Doc had in the freezer, as well as some bread. With a salad and cheese, we had a meal. The afternoon had turned chilly with a northwesterly breeze. Ty lit a fire. We ate and were warm, and each, in our own way, grateful. J reached over to me and grasped my hand tightly in the middle of the meal. Ty passed a Tylenol bottle as if it were some ceremonial part of the meal. We all began to laugh in spite of ourselves.

"I think that since we're all here in one room, we should compare stories. I know some parts, but I have a lot of things I'm curious about," suggested Doc.

Grunts of satisfaction and agreement resounded throughout the group. We tried to make ourselves as comfortable as possible in the large living room. I passed out the ice packs while Dad stoked up the fire.

As he went to his seat, Randall paused, looking at Doc. "I guess I should start, because something I found out got this thing rolling." I remembered Red's disclosure of last night. What could this be about?

"My job at the State Department brings me in contact with a lot of information about terrorist activities. When we arrange meetings between heads of state, I have to protect these guys. I have to know which terrorist organizations are ticked off at which prime ministers, princes, kings, presidents, etc."

I was beginning to see the light.

"About three weeks ago," he continued, "I received a memo from our office in New York, describing a tip received about a bomb factory. We've been investigating it ever since."

"How did J get involved?" I asked.

"The New York Police Department stumbled on the bomb factory by accident. They were tracking down a series of hit-and-run accidents. When they found the van responsible, the Department of Motor Vehicles came up with an Ali Mahmut. He turned out to be an illegal alien. That brought the Feds in, who staked out Ali's residence. The surveillance men became suspicious when they began to notice the packages and materials going in and out."

"How could they tell it was a bomb factory from the packages?" asked Ty. "These guys aren't dumb. They must've disguised the packages."

"Right. These surveillance agents are quite experienced," Randall answered, looking around at the faces now riveted by his story.

"Carelessly, the men had forgotten to destroy one of the packing slips and a label with a SKU number. We traced it and came up with a load of materials commonly used by bomb makers, materials that, by themselves, are harmless, but in the right combination, well—*kaboom*.

"We also had the packing materials chemically analyzed for any residue. That was even better evidence. These tests proved positive for Semtex. The bomb makers get this stuff from illegal suppliers. Unfortunately, there is a big underground marketplace out there for these materials. There's probably a special chapter for the suppliers in the terrorists' handbook. The bottom line is that this was an active bomb factory, which meant that they were planning a terrorist action very soon. You can't store many of these unstable chemicals. It's too dangerous, and if the place is raided, you don't want to leave this kind of evidence lying around."

"Why didn't you just wait until they were all inside the residence and raid them?" asked Alice.

"Because we knew that they were being supplied by someone," he replied. "We wanted to get as many of them as possible. So often when there is a raid in a terrorist's house, enough of them elude the dragnet, and they just form another house somewhere else."

"That's when Randy contacted my division," J picked up the story. "We handle all kinds of special assignments. Our job was to find out where they were getting their supplies. We traced them to the Ocean Beach ferry."

"How did you become their contact?" asked Doc. "That had to be tricky. To be honest, I had no idea that you were working when you came out here. I was already suspicious with regard to our neighbors. I managed to get some candid shots of them on the cottage porch using a very good camera and sent them off to my old buddies in the CIA. I received the names and a brief dossier on each of them the day after Jill left here. Secretly, I was proud of myself. I had their number from the get-go."

Ty sat with his head bent, hands clasped and hanging between his legs. "When I get back on campus, I want to go see Professor Taled. I feel so sad for him. He truly is a man with a vision for peace. A great mind. Maybe I can offer him some comfort."

Randall cautioned, "You will be asked to make a statement by all the law enforcement agencies involved and advised on what you can and cannot say to him, Ty. I'm really sorry. I know how you feel. But, Professor Taled and his home and loved ones will be watched until his son is caught."

Doc continued, "I reported back to the CIA/NY office, and they connected me with Red, who wanted all the information. But like any good man in his field, he never mentioned a word about Jill. I didn't know she was involved."

He looked at her, and she picked up the story.

"My chance came when the CIA sent my division all the information on terrorist activities known to them in the area. There was a woman, Karen Eig, a German from a defunct terrorist cell proven to be connected to the bombing of two passenger jets. She seemed to disappear. She was either dead or had gone deeply underground to enable her to work with another terrorist cell whose identity was yet unknown to our intelligence community.

"I took a real chance, and it didn't pay off. The two guys in the cottage didn't suspect anything. But, when my contact from the first day on the ferry met me, he got suspicious. I had retrieved two shipments for them by the time he checked me out with his people. I thought I had pulled it off. But he came back two nights ago and asked some questions that I didn't have answers for. These were details of her terrorist career that only Karen Eig and a close associate would know. He talked to that close associate, who showed him a photo. My cover was blown, and they had to get rid of me. They had the materials they needed, and I was too dangerous.

"I didn't know when I planned this vacation that I'd have to mix business with pleasure," said J ruefully. "I feel like I shortchanged Annie." She must have seen how hurt I was by the look on my face.

"The man you spoke to on the ferry trip that first day was your contact, wasn't he?" I wanted to confirm my suspicions. I didn't want to hear that this vacation was part of one of J's assignments.

"Your instincts are very good, my Annie. He was the contact. I felt that we had been as careful as careful could be, but time was of the essence."

"Oh, J, how careful were you?" I asked. "You got caught!" The anger kept the tears from flowing.

"Yes. I took a really big chance and wish I had coordinated better with our intelligence people at CIA and FBI. It was the time factor. If we wanted to get them, it had to be that moment, that slim margin of time."

"They were getting nervous, anyway. Alice was snooping. Ty and Annie kept running into them at inopportune times. They would have pulled out in a couple of days anyway," added Doc.

"Yes, we were lucky to finger as many of them as we did," mused J, shifting painfully in her chair.

"But no one is in jail. They're all still out there," I protested.

"Our big chance will come tomorrow. Our president is planning a secret meeting with Middle Eastern leaders aboard a ship right outside the Fire Island Inlet. We think this may be their target. We're waiting for them." Randall's explanation left the group quiet and tense. We contemplated the gravity of this situation.

"We have photographs of all of them. They will not be able to get past security," said J.

"But what if they bring in someone you don't know? That seems an obvious trick for terrorists to pull," asked Alice.

"That's true," said Randall. "We'll be waiting. The explosives J delivered to them are laced with a mineral that can be picked up by our security X-ray machines."

"We have plenty of evidence against them when we catch them," said Doc. "The crime scene unit lifted a set of prints from *Star* when she was stolen that one night."

"Plus, we can identify them. They confessed that they had a bomb factory to Ty and me," I added.

"We're also waiting for a set of prints from the key ring," added Doc.

"Wouldn't the water wash them away?" asked Ty.

"Not necessarily. Remember, fingerprints have oil. Not so easy to wash off in water," J responded.

The phone rang. Doc went into the kitchen to answer it.

"I'm going to bed," said J.

No one protested, as we all began to stir from our comfy chairs, gathering up our belongings.

Doc returned with a look of satisfaction. "The arson investigation by NYPD shows that there was a timed device used to set the fire at the cottage. It is the same kind as those used by our little terrorist group. No matter what happens tomorrow, they'll go away for a long time for arson and attempted murder."

"It's nice to see all these loose ends coming together," Ty murmured, stifling a yawn, hardly able to keep his eyes opened.

"Speaking of loose ends," Alice piped in, coming alive, "when I get my mail tomorrow, we'll have an answer about the Madonna Ghost. The young man who takes in my mail said there is a letter from the Historical Society."

I felt a flutter of excitement. Not a strong one though. I was too tired. I turned to say good night and caught J giving Alice the strangest look.

"I can't wait to hear what you found out, Alice," she said.

"Tomorrow, you'll have to tell me what you guys were doing while I was otherwise tied up." she quipped.

As I walked back to my room with J and Randall, I wondered about Alice's letter. I had forgotten about the Madonna Ghost.

Chapter 17

ALICE AND THE GHOST

WE WERE LYING ON THE soft white sand. Everyone had slept late, and the two of us slipped out of the house to lie quietly together. No phone calls. No depositions to be given to detectives. J was tucked safely in her room. I didn't have to worry about her. My dad was here, so I didn't have to avoid his phone calls. If we were lucky, the folks at Windalee would find our note and not call out the National Guard when we weren't in the kitchen for a group breakfast.

"Ty?" I said it softly so I wouldn't wake him if he were sleeping. Both our eyes were blackened today from our head injuries. We looked like raccoon twins.

"Um, what?" he mumbled.

"I had it out with my father when he arrived at Windalee yesterday," I started.

"Annie, what does that mean, you had it out?" he asked.

"Ty, I'm not as far along with this as you are. You must have had times when you weren't so patient with your dad." I felt the sting of hurt at his remark.

"I told him that I resented being hounded about my mother. I also told him that I resented his being away so much."

"What did he say?"

"He said he'd back off," I replied.

"How did that sit with you?"

"I feel relieved, Ty. I will call him. I do love him. I know he can't help it that his job takes him away. I just resent him trying to run things from the Arab Emirates or wherever he happens to be at that moment."

"It's that simple?" Ty asked. I could hear the doubt in his voice.

"No. He makes me feel guilty. I love living with J. He has to work, travel, and take care of my mother. I'm out of it. Every time he calls, I realize that I'm not doing anything to help him. But, I don't know what I'm supposed to be doing."

"Um, yeah, that takes time," he grunted again, turning his well-done side away from the sun. He sat up to put on a T-shirt and threw me one.

"You're getting red," he observed. "I'm going to visit my dad tomorrow, if the police don't need us," he announced. "I'm going to bring some old family pictures for him to look at. He might like that." I could picture Ty showing photos to his father.

I thought about what it might be like to sit with my mother in the rec room at the rehab, going through old photos. It was the first time I had thought about being with her in a long time.

"Let's go back to Windalee." Ty rose and offered me his hand. He helped me up and pulled me to him, kissing me for a long gentle moment.

"There," he said. "That was pretty good, Annie. Neither one of us screamed in pain. I think this relationship might survive our injuries." I laughed, and we strolled back to the house.

Everyone was in Doc's kitchen. The aroma of his wonderful coffee filled the room.

"Hi, Lt. Red."

"Red, what's the news from the mainland?" Doc called over his shoulder. He was frying up some omelets.

"I'm hungry," I said, succumbing to the smell of the kitchen.

Doc showed us all to the table. We sat down to eat while Red filled us in.

"We got the results of the fingerprint ID from the key chain," he offered, his blue eyes twinkling with satisfaction.

"Well," urged Alice.

"One set of prints match the prints from the *Star*. That gives us a positive ID for one of them."

"I wonder if it's Tattoo or Tall One."

Red turned to me at that comment. "You're going to tell us, Annie." He produced a manila envelope from which he pulled some police file photos.

"That's him." Ty was the first to pick Tattoo out of the group of mean-looking men in the photos. "And that's Tall One," I added, pointing out another picture.

"Any idea where they are?" Doc inquired.

"The bomb factory has been abandoned," Red replied. "So we lost them temporarily. We hope to pick them up again in the vicinity of Bay Shore. All the Secret Service guarding any access point to the president have been alerted. Now, I can give them pictures of who to look for."

"I can't believe that they could get to the president," I protested.

"History would prove you wrong," commented Red. "There have been plenty of assassinations, three of them American presidents."

The group grew silent, as they contemplated this dismal observation.

A salutation came from the back door, "Alice, I have your mail."

A boy of about ten years came into the kitchen, as I held the door for him. He handed a packet of envelopes to Alice.

"Thanks, Brian," she said. "Can you stay for breakfast?"

"Oh, no. Thanks. Mom wants me home," and he excused himself.

Alice quickly leafed through the envelopes, seizing one. "This is from my friend at the Historical Society," she proclaimed. "It should contain their verdict about the stone we found in the tunnel."

"What's this all about?" J asked. We filled her in on our adventures in pursuit of the Madonna Ghost while she was playing terrorist.

"Tell me more about what you saw on the beach. What did this apparition look like?" J was serious in her curiosity. I didn't think she would be so interested in a ghost.

Alice was more than happy to tell J everything she had found about our ghost.

"The most interesting thing about the apparition was her appearance as she emerged from the water." Alice was warming to the subject.

"How so?" J probed again.

"She seemed to glow from the inside. She had on a long shroud-like garment, and a glow seemed to emanate from her."

"Yes. All three of us saw the same thing," Ty added.

"This is my first ghost. So, I guess nothing surprised me." I really hadn't thought about our ghost for the last day. Come to think of it, she was an awesome ghost. She walked. She glowed. She disappeared.

"Our theory was that she disappeared by the cottage, because she was looking for something. We convinced Doc to let us explore the tunnel between Windalee and the cottage."

"I tried to discourage you folks from going anywhere near the cottage. I was convinced by that time that our neighbors were what I'd like to call unsavory at the very least," said Doc.

"When we found what we thought was a grave marker in the tunnel, we felt that the Madonna Ghost was returning to the graveyard where she and her child had been buried," I continued.

"Hot dog!" Alice whooped, almost upsetting her wheelchair.

"Alice, calm down!" I teased her. "What does the letter say?"

She read to us:

Dear Miss D'Elia,

With regards to the stone you sent to us for authenticity, we are pleased to tell you that our forensic and historical analyses have indeed identified the piece as a grave marker of the period you have indicated. Using special X-ray photography, we were able to raise the names and dates on the stone. They are Anna and Miep Von Thaden.

Furthermore, our historian has been able to validate your records concerning the Von Thaden family. You have most decidedly located the grave of the mother and child in question.

If you should need to examine the remains for further authentication, I have included information regarding the appropriate legal procedures.

I hope we have been of service. We will be contacting you about acquiring further information to fill in our records here at the society.

"I feel this information can bring this poor woman to peace

somehow," Alice added quietly, the jubilation of her successful research replaced by some budding idea.

"I hate to do this," said J, "but this is too serious to let you go on thinking you've seen a real ghost."

Astonishment filled us. "What are you talking about, J? You weren't there. You didn't see her. How do you know she wasn't real?" Really, I thought J was going to try to give us some scientific explanation of something she hadn't seen herself. I gestured us all to be quiet. She looked at us levelly.

"Annie. Everyone. I was your ghost."

Silence filled the room.

"Please explain yourself," Alice requested.

"My job as a terrorist was to swim out through the surf and rendezvous with a package dropped from a boat. The package had raw materials for explosives."

"Swim out for a package?" I asked.

"How were you supposed to find it at night?"

"One, it transmitted a radio signal to a tiny waterproof receiver I carried. Two, it had a powerful light on it. Then I took it up to the cottage."

"Not too dangerous, J," I mumbled, a knot of fear in my stomach. Sometimes, I couldn't believe the crazy things she did. Jill continued her story.

"I left a blanket on the beach. One, because it was cold after my little swim. Two, if I ran into anyone, I had to hide the package. I couldn't get the beeper from the last shipment to go off. You must have seen me walking up to the cottage with the package under the blanket. I would drop the whole load into a depression in the yard, which I now see was the old tunnel entrance. Then I would sneak off to the back of the cottage. I thought I looked a little weird, but I didn't think I'd end up as somebody's ghost. Sorry." Jill looked from one to the other of us.

"It makes sense, Jill," said Alice thoughtfully.

Alice surprised me. I thought she would be more emotional about finding out that the ghost wasn't real. She seemed to have read my mind.

"Jill, how many trips from the surf to the cottage did you make?"

"Only two. They did the drop off when there was no moon," Jill replied.

"But you see, I've seen Madonna Ghost on other moonless nights. She never had the light though. I've been trying to figure out that glow. What its significance was. Now I know. None."

"I've seen her, too," said Ty, "with Alice."

"How odd that you should end up following the same path taken by our ghost." Alice seemed to be trying to attach some significance to Jill's being mistaken for the ghost.

"I wonder if Madonna Ghost was trying to protect you, Jill?" she said. "She must have been upset that sick, evil people were near the grave of her beloved child."

"I don't know, Alice. Maybe she was my guardian angel. Maybe she did lead you to me."

"You know, Jill, I did find your earring back in the tunnel," I exclaimed, having forgotten all about it in the turmoil of the last forty-eight hours. "The one that matched the earring I found outside the cottage. How did the earring get back into the tunnel?"

"They must have taken me into the tunnel at some point," answered J. "They hit me with a hypodermic needle as soon as I couldn't come up with the name for the operation. I guess that's when I lost the earring."

"That could explain the large package I saw them hauling through the backyard of the cottage," Alice murmured.

"It seems too much of a coincidence that the earring back and the grave marker were found at the same time," she added.

"What are you saying, Alice?" I asked.

"Some spirits are benign. I think she guided us, helped us to find J. I don't believe in coincidence." Alice looked up at us.

"I want to put Madonna Ghost to rest. When I get the grave marker back from the Historical Society, I want to place the marker in the cottage garden and establish it as the formal grave of Anna Von Thaden and her child."

"I'd like to be there, Alice," said J. "I think I might owe the lady."

"Me too," came the almost simultaneous response from the members of our group.

Chapter 18
THE GHOST GOES HOME

THE NEXT MORNING, I AWOKE to the slam of a door at Windalee. The small clock on my night stand said six. *That was Lt. Red and Dad, off to catch the terrorists,* I thought.

This was the day of the president's summit meeting. This was the day that the forces of good (my dad and Lt. Red) would thwart the forces of evil (Tattoo and Tall One). I'd best get up and catch the event.

I had a long hot shower, indulging in the dubious luxury of sorting out my thoughts. It was the first time that I had been alone to do this. I was so grateful that J was safe again, for how long, I didn't know. I was also satisfied with the new arrangement with my father.

And then, there was Ty. *Would I see him after this vacation?* I wondered if our promise to stay in touch would hold. I felt so close to him. I tried to think of not having him there to talk to. Well, of course, this was going to happen. I had to go home. He had to go off to college. But would we continue our friendship? Life's uncertainties. What would I do without them?

I put on some clean clothes and headed for the kitchen. Everyone was there, glued to the TV. The lead story was a visit by a rock group from Moscow.

"Why is everyone watching the TV? The president's meeting is a secret," I asked.

"If there's an assassination attempt, it won't be a secret," answered Doc, passing me a muffin and coffee.

"Oh. That's pretty grim," I observed.

"So right," agreed Ty. "Feel like a walk, Annie?

"Um." I nodded with a mixture of dread and enthusiasm. All of a sudden, it was hard to swallow the muffin I'd been wolfing down a minute ago. We walked along the familiar boardwalk, heading for the sand. Ty was unusually quiet.

"Why so glum?" I asked, the fear and uncertainty of what I had been thinking squeezing at my heart.

"Annie, when are you leaving?" Ty asked, turning to me.

"What?" I gasped, searching his face for the meaning of his words.

"I mean …" He paused, unable to say what was on his mind. "What are we going to do about us? When you have to go home, when I have to go to school, I mean. I want to see you again," came the rush of words.

I exhaled a long releasing sigh. "I thought you were going to visit me in the 'big city,' Ty," I offered.

"Annie, I do want you to e-mail me at school." He looked at me hopefully.

"Of course I will write to you. I can't afford the phone bill, otherwise," I gulped, my heart swelling as the icy fingers of insecurity let go.

He grinned his gorgeous grin, got up, and held me to him. "This is going to be hard, Annie. I'm going to miss you."

"Me too, Ty. You're very special to me now. I feel that we're connected. Let's promise to meet as soon as we can." We hugged for a long moment.

"We should go back," Ty said.

At that moment, we heard a dull rumble. We looked at each other. "We'd best be getting back."

As we walked, I felt as if I had left my old self behind. The fear was gone. I had Ty, and he had me. I felt a connection I had never experienced before. We started to walk back in silence. At last, Ty asked,

"I wonder if that noise was significant and when we'll find out if our favorite thugs have been caught?"

"Never. If we don't get back in that kitchen with the rest of the crowd," I joked.

We took the rest of the way back to Windalee very slowly, knowing it might be the last walk for some time. J and I would leave in the morning for the city. The kitchen was quite a different scene this time. There was much animated conversation. But as the commercial on the TV ended and the face of the news commentator returned, loud shushing squelched the conversation.

The grim face on the TV delivered this message, "There was an explosion off the coast of Fire Island about twenty minutes ago. The Suffolk County marine police have been joined by the FBI in their investigation, posing many questions as to the cause of the blast. Drugs and terrorism are the two major areas of speculation. Stay tuned for more details."

"Has anyone heard from Lt. Red or my dad?" I asked, beginning to become concerned, not even wanting to think that they might have been in the blast.

"No," answered J.

"What have they said on the TV?" I pressed.

"Just what you've heard."

"How close was the explosion to the summit meeting?" Ty asked.

"From the look of the map on the news show, within a mile, about fifteen miles offshore, I'd say," replied J.

"Do they know if it was a boat, or what?" I was beginning to feel panic rising.

The TV program was interrupted again. "More on the Fire Island explosion," the commentator announced. "The debris around the site of the explosion reveals that it occurred on a small fishing boat. Police are searching for wreckage pieces that might lead to information regarding the ownership of the craft. Stay tuned for continuing coverage of this late-breaking story."

The phone rang. Doc answered it. Everyone stared, not daring to breathe. After an interminable thirty seconds, he said, "Yes, Lieutenant. Thanks very much," and hung up.

"They're okay," he smiled triumphantly, freeing us from our frozen state.

"What about the explosion?" Alice started the barrage of questions.

"Was anyone on the boat?" J pressed.

"Did the explosives belong to the terrorists?" Ty wanted to know.

Doc raised his hand for silence. "The explosion was the bomb that our two friends were aiming at the presidential yacht. They had a homing device set on the launch that blew up. It was headed for the target device that had been placed on the yacht by one of the terrorists. He got onboard disguised as a member of the food service staff. However, those explosives were removed by our bomb people after we alerted them."

Alice butted in, asking the question we were all dying to hear the answer to. "Did they get Tattoo and Tall One?"

"Tattoo was apprehended leaving the bomb factory. There was a car chase. He ditched the car when he got stuck in traffic and was brought down by a bullet in the leg. Tall One is missing. According to Tattoo, he never showed up. There's a heightened security alert at all points of exit from the U.S."

"But we know that here on Long Island, all he needs is a boat, and he can rendezvous with a ship offshore. I fear we haven't heard the last of him," Doc answered.

The faces around the room registered disappointment and tension. J spoke for us all. "This man is a danger to us and our nation. They must get him!"

Doc continued, "At least Tattoo will be put away for a long time and perhaps give us some information about Fareed Taled, aka Tall One, in exchange for some leniency."

There were nods and grunts of approval from us all. The mood had turned somber.

The phone jangled, and Doc went to answer it. The rest of us looked on expectantly. Good news or bad?

Doc listened, head bent to the phone, nodding intently, and then, hung up. He returned with a face that could only be described as cynical disbelief and awe.

"The bomb factory experienced a minor explosion followed by an intense fire, according to witnesses. The police are sifting through the debris. According to the police, all explosives were removed, so this has to be arson, but how and by whom?"

"These men are incredibly dangerous and clever. Their motivation to make a point fuels them to be successful in their mission." J knew her terrorists.

Doc continued to fill in the details. "The bomb factory was heavily guarded and thoroughly searched before the fire. Knowing how Tall One pulled this off is going to depend on the results of the arson investigation. But a preliminary investigation reveals that there are no human remains."

"As far as we can see, Tall One is on the run. His capture will be top priority for the intelligence community around the world."

J shivered, and in spite of what fears she might have about the return of Fareed Taled, she raised her glass and called for a toast.

"To us! May we keep up the good fight!"

"Hear! Hear!" we cried.

The group returned to their speculative conversations, leaving Ty and me to make plans about where we could meet again.

Alice clapped her hands over the noise, signaling for our attention. "Now that our ghost has been identified, I think it would be a wonderful act of kindness to formally lay her to rest," she announced.

"Yes, I agree," said J. "I feel I owe her some loving gesture. I'd like to believe that she was my guardian angel."

"Certainly, if Alice had not been so interested in her, we would have never been on the beach that night, and seen our ghost," Ty added.

"I'm for it," Doc agreed. "It's the right thing to do. Her grave has been disturbed too many times. I'd like to place a permanent marker right here in my garden, if all agree."

"The Historical Society will have to be consulted," Alice pointed out. "But I don't see why they wouldn't agree. As long as you don't mind putting the original grave marker in your memorial as well," she said.

"Not at all," murmured Doc.

"Will we have to wait for the marker to be returned from the Historical Society?" I asked. "J and I are leaving tomorrow. I hoped we could have the little ceremony before we go."

"Yes. Me too," agreed J.

"We could have that little ceremony tonight," Alice offered. "Your father will be here by then, won't he, Annie?"

"Yes, that's right," J smiled. "We all should be here. It would be so nice."

"At sundown, then. It's settled." Alice seemed very pleased. "Ty, I need some stuff for the ceremony from my house. Can you get it for me?" Ty agreed.

The rest of the afternoon was taken up with the trivia of wrapping up a vacation. Ty, Doc, and Alice prepared for the ceremony. J supervised as I packed. Dad and Lt. Red arrived from the ferry.

At sunset we made our way to the beach. I thought about how much I would miss this place when we leave tomorrow. The breeze was brisk, blowing from the ocean, bearing with it the smell of salt and the call of seabirds.

Except for a few puffs in the west, the sky was a seamless blue, the horizon visible in every direction. We were trapped inside a vast blue violet bowl, inverted over us by an unknown giant. The warm sea breeze lifted sheets of sand, rippling the white expanse of the beach.

Tonight the surf was a gentle swell, curling into the shore, fringing it with foam. Alice had asked us to gather by the edge of the ocean for our small tribute. She said that was where the Madonna Ghost felt her greatest pain, was most restless. It was here, she offered, that we might best put her to rest.

"Alice picked a good night for the ceremony," Ty observed. "It's so peaceful. A real gentle night."

"I hope we do give her some peace," I responded. "Placing the gravestone in a permanent garden by the walkway is a lovely idea."

The sound of a motor bored its way into the peace. A large three-wheeled bike, driven by Doc, chugged into view, pulling a service cart with Alice and J in it.

"That's right!" I exclaimed, slapping my head. "I never thought about how they would get down here. Neither of them is walking too well."

Ty chuckled. "Doc: ever the inventive one."

The last crescent of the sun's fireball dipped below the horizon as if on cue, giving our funeral an eerie light. J propped herself against the service cart, while Alice remained inside, handing out a large wreath.

"I have a reading I'd like to do," she announced, showing us a book Ty had fetched from Glass House.

"We thought we'd toss this wreath into the surf," J declared. "Doc says the tide will take it out."

My dad came around the other side of me. Alice gestured for us to form a circle. We joined hands. With Ty's strong hand on my left and my dad's on the right, I felt light as air. Across from me in our circle, J was backlit by the remaining light from the sunset. Her hair, blowing gently around her head, glowed like a halo. Alice began to read.

"For a mother's love for her child. For a child's trust in its mother. For peace from pain. For succor from injury. May the lady who walks these shores find her heavenly rest. May she join that babe whom she seeks to revive.

"May she know that her child has lain peacefully in the arms of angels and that her child calls her to join them. Listen, sweet mother. Hear your baby's call. Go toward the light. Your baby waits for you beyond the light. Go and rest with her. She calls to you."

Alice paused, bowing her head. "Let us pray," she intoned. We bowed our heads, willing the Madonna Ghost to go home to her baby. My hands felt one with the two I held. I couldn't feel the sand beneath my feet. My eyes were tightly closed, so there was no warning for what was about to happen.

A warm wind swirled around us, starting at our feet, whipping the sand. I opened my eyes but had to shut them quickly, because sand grains flew everywhere. We were enveloped in whirlpools of the swirling stuff. I thought about running, but it wouldn't happen.

Then it was over. The air became still again. I opened my eyes. It had become dark, with stars quite visible against a black sky. We looked up, as one, the circle still joined. At that moment, a meteor entered the atmosphere, and a shooting star glittered briefly across the blackness.

"Let's take that for a sign that she's gone," breathed Alice, breaking the spell.

Breinigsville, PA USA
05 April 2011
259227BV00001B/7/P